"You're a wise woman, Mary."

"Not so wise. Sometimes it's easier to give advice than to take it."

"Nevertheless. . ." He pushed himself up from the steps and gazed down at her.

She was so beautiful, so pale and lovely, so fragile in the moonlight. And yet he knew that beneath the apparent fragility was a strong, passionate, independent spirit. Mary Smith was a competent woman who was nevertheless capable of deep compassion and tenderness, as he'd witnessed with his son, Timmy.

The duality of her nature intrigued and attracted him in a way that he'd never experienced before.

As he looked down at her now, she quite literally took his breath away.

Suddenly stunned at the direction his thoughts were taking, he turned abruptly. "I'd probably better go home before Timmy has another one of his night walks."

"Oh my. Indeed you should. Where has the time gone?"

He reached down to help her up. "Though I'm not too worried. He hasn't had one of those episodes since you came into his life."

She was standing now and quite steady. Still, he couldn't seem to make himself release her.

Foolish, foolish, he thought, as the smooth softness of her small white hand engaged his senses.

"You've been a good friend, Mary," he said gruffly. "Your— your husband is a lucky man."

He shouldn't have said that, either. He knew it, but the words just came out.

And she didn't withdraw her hand. Not immediately.

RACHEL DRUTEN is a native Californian. She is an artist as well as an author, wife, mother, and grandmother. Much of her time is devoted to overseeing a nonprofit, on-site, after-school program in the arts for disadvantaged children in grades K through 5.

Books by Rachel Druten

HEARTSONG PRESENTS

Alias, Mary Smith

Rachel Druten

Heartsong Presents

This book is lovingly dedicated to my family and friends, and to Berta, all of whom have made my passion to write possible.

I would be remiss in not again acknowledging my quadrumvirate of editors, dear friends: Dianna Crawford, Sheila Herron and Barbara Wilder, and my husband, Charles, always willing to wield his red pencil.

And, with a most grateful heart, I thank my editors, JoAnne Simmons and Debra Peterson, for their continued understanding, patience, and encouragement.

A note from the Author:
I love to hear from my readers! You may correspond with me by writing:

Rachel Druten
Author Relations
PO Box 721
Uhrichsville, OH 44683

ISBN 978-1-60260-190-1

ALIAS, MARY SMITH

All scripture quotations are taken from the King James Version of the Bible.

All of the characters and events in this book are fictitious. Any resemblance to actual persons, living or dead, or to actual events is purely coincidental.

Our mission is to publish and distribute inspirational products offering exceptional value and biblical encouragement to the masses.

PRINTED IN THE U.S.A.

prologue

Marybelle Rockford surveyed the opulent bedroom.

She wouldn't miss it. None of it!

Hurriedly she snapped the satchel shut. Beneath her lace undergarments lay her escape from Clayton—the money she'd saved from selling her fine jewelry. Only a few pieces were left, packed in the bottom, keepsakes from her parents, long gone.

Brushing aside a dark curl, she touched the scar running down her cheek, almost indiscernible now, but every time she looked into the mirror, she remembered the bloody red gash from Clayton's ring when he'd hit her, really hit her for the first time.

And her limp, though slight, a constant reminder of the time he had pushed her down the stairs in a drunken rage.

She glanced at the clock.

After midnight.

The servants had retired to their quarters. By now her *devoted* husband should be well into his cups at the local gambling club. Heaven only knew what time he would finally decide to come home tonight.

But it didn't matter. By then she would be gone.

No, she wouldn't miss those nights when he dragged himself in at dawn and threw himself next to her on the bed, drunk and demanding. She would not miss his groping hands and hot breath thick with the stench of whiskey and tobacco.

Suddenly the enormity of what she was about to do hit her. Her pulse quickened. Fear made her weak. The same fear that had kept her shackled to him these past three years.

But no more!

She took a moment to lay her hand upon the new life growing large beneath her loosely flowing dress. . .this new, new life that had instilled her with courage. She would not let her baby suffer Clayton's violent rages as she had.

She slipped into her scarlet fur-lined cloak. "Merry Christmas, Clayton," she muttered, swinging the satchel from the bed.

"So, what have we here?"

The voice, rough and slurring, blasted from behind her.

Marybelle whirled around.

Clayton!

He swayed in the doorway. His insolent gaze slid over her. "As if I have to ask." He stepped forward, a demonic smile lacing his voluptuous lips, a chilling contrast to the fury flaming in his rheumy gray eyes.

Her blood turned to ice. She stood frozen, unable to move, as slowly, unsteadily, he advanced, until he stood over her, menacing in sheer bulk and brute strength.

Without warning, his fist shot out, aimed straight for her baby. Reactively she swung to the side. The blow, glancing off her belly, sent her sprawling back onto the bed.

Roaring expletives, he threw himself on the bed next to her. Gripping the collar of her cloak, he pushed his face close, so close she could feel his searing breath against her lips, smell the acrid odor of sweat and drink.

"I have a sixth sense about you, Marybelle," he snarled. "You've been too nice of late. Something had to be up."

Gasping for air, she twisted from his grip and rolled off the bed onto the floor below him. He groped out for her, but she dodged aside. Struggling to her knees, she began to crawl toward the bedroom door.

"Why you little. . ." Catching her foot, he rose, dragging her up. "You think you can get away?" His eyes were glazed with a white-hot fury as he raised his fist, slammed it across her mouth. She tasted the salt of blood.

The room went dark.

No! She couldn't faint.

He grabbed a handful of her hair, jerking her up.

Blindly she reached toward the bedside table, grasping for anything, anything to protect her—to protect her baby—from his rage.

The porcelain figurine crashed to the floor. The vase of roses tumbled—shattered.

Her hand clamped around the small Tiffany lamp with its heavy metal base.

And swung!

She heard the cracking thud as it made impact with the side of his skull.

A howl of pain and rage rasped from his lips as he fell backward, clutching his head.

Struggling to her feet, she hit him again.

And again! And again!

She had no idea how many times she struck him. All she knew was that her arm ached and she felt as if her lungs would burst.

She was aware of the clatter of the lamp hitting the floor. She stood up, bathed in sweat.

In the light of the companion lamp, her husband lay sprawled on the bed, tangled in the coverlet, the sheets crimson with his blood.

She wiped her own sticky hands down the sides of her scarlet cloak. She had no time for guilt or remorse. She had to escape.

She grabbed the precious satchel and hurried down the spiral staircase. Quiet now, quiet so as not to draw the attention of any servants awakened by the commotion. Down the stairs and across the marble floor of the entry hall. She unlatched the great double doors.

The satchel was heavy with the weight of the money—but light with the hope of her freedom.

She skirted the house and ran across the rear yard to the stable where Simon waited—her old groom, the only one in whom she had confided. The only one who knew of her plan and had willingly volunteered to help her.

No doubt Clayton had left his horse in the stable when he'd returned. No doubt the groom had seen the drunken lout stagger into the house.

She would not tell the old man what had transpired within. He would find out soon enough.

Earlier he'd put her trunk on the back floorboard of the phaeton. He had harnessed the mare. Now, silently, he took the satchel from her trembling hand and placed it beside the trunk, then he helped her hoist her unwieldy body up onto the seat.

Impulsively she leaned toward him and gave his weathered cheek a kiss. They both knew this would be the last time they would meet. That he would never see the child she would soon give birth to—the child whose life he might be saving.

Without a word, he led the horse from the stable and turned her toward the road.

Marybelle flicked the reins, cracking the whip above her stylish mare's flank. The sleek hackney lunged forward and broke into a run, racing down the long, cedar-lined drive.

As the phaeton careened onto the road, she glanced back. A small light still glowed in the corner bedroom window upstairs.

one

Even in the shrouded silence of the fog, she imagined she could hear his footfall, feel his hot breath on her cheek.

Heart pounding, she blindly pushed through the thick underbrush, stumbling over rocks, knocking against the trunks of trees and into bushes, her feet sinking into the spongy loam as she ran.

Her chest burned. Her legs trembled with terror and fatigue. Branches scratched her face; nettles snagged her gown. In the chill air, she drew her cloak closer, cradling her baby beneath it, warming her, protecting her.

Suddenly she stumbled and lurched forward. The infant cried out in fear.

"Hush, my little one," her desperate whisper soft as the surrounding fog. "Please don't cry."

Then his hand clamped her shoulder.

Caught!

He swung her around, and her own silent screams clogged in her throat.

And the baby cried and cried and would not stop.

❧

Mary woke, shivering in the frigid sweat of relief, her flannel nightgown damp and clinging. Her infant nestled in the crook of her arm, weeping.

"Shh." She pressed her cheek against the downy-soft head. "We're safe now."

Even if they were never found, would they ever be truly safe? Not from the nightmares. Not from the memories. . . that horrible night she had fled, her child, yet to be born, growing beneath her heart.

She pulled the small precious bundle to her, suckling baby

Nancy against her breast, stroking her until the tiny fist that clenched around her finger loosened and her child fell again into untroubled slumber.

She must put the memories behind her, erase them from her mind. She was Mary Smith now.

Mary Smith.

But her demons of night would not be so easily commanded. She stared into the dark, imagining she could hear his hoarse cry, his arms stretched out, blood streaming down his face.

"Help me. For God's sake, help me."

She imagined his hand clutching at her skirt, saw herself stepping over his helpless body and fleeing down the spiral staircase.

Not until her infant stirred again and she heard the clock strike one, could she allow herself to sleep.

❧

Mary lit a match and turned up the kerosene lamp in the small but efficient kitchen. She glanced at the clock sitting on top of the pie cooler. It was just after four in the morning.

Her sleep had been spasmodic and fitful, like so many nights, filled with troubled dreams. Rather than entertain them or stare for hours into the dark in morbid rumination, she had gotten into the habit of getting up and making herself a cup of tea. There was something she found comforting in the ritual.

She stoked the wood-burning stove, filled the kettle at the sink and put it on the iron plate. While she waited for the water to boil, she spooned leaves into the teapot, drew a delicately fluted and flowered cup and saucer from the cupboard, and sat down at the kitchen table.

Cocking her elbow on the table, she rested her chin on her fist as she absently glanced around the well-appointed kitchen. Everything she needed was close at hand, unlike her mansion in Chicago where the kitchen would have taken half the space of this lovely cottage's first floor. But of course, it had been designed for a staff of servants, not just a single homemaker like herself.

And in this remote little town, hers was one of the few cottages with piped-in water. Such a blessing! Especially now with a baby, when she could use every bit of help she could get.

At the very time she was searching for a safe haven for herself and Nancy, old Mrs. Armitage had died.

The woman's daughter, Agnes, who, by all accounts, had been almost a slave to the old lady, was out of there almost before the body was cold—gone east to marry the man who'd "not been good enough for her" in the mean old woman's lifetime. Agnes had hooked up the horse, hopped in the carriage, and left. No keepsakes, just a small satchel and the clothes on her back.

Sold to the first bidder, which was Mary, the house was a two-story Queen Anne cottage, in perfect condition and perfectly furnished, even to the linens and a silver service and place settings for twelve. An irony, for it was said that Mrs. Armitage, the richest person in town, never entertained but would set out her treasures to admire and have Agnes polish.

It was easy to see why Agnes never wanted to set eyes on any of it again, but for Mary, it was a boon.

She hadn't needed one thing to settle in: not a napkin, not a pot, not a pillow or a lace coverlet. The only thing she'd needed was a crib for Nancy.

There was even a stable for Queenie, her mare, and a carriage house for her stylish phaeton with a room above for Hitch Chapell, the caretaker she'd inherited with the cottage.

All she lacked was a cook and a housekeeper. But now, on her limited budget, those were skills she would have to learn. Not that Aunt Hannah, who had brought her up, hadn't taught her the rudiments: "If you're going to direct servants, you absolutely must know what is sensible to expect."

At twenty-two, she had already lived three lives: as Marybelle Clairborn, the doted-on only child of wealthy parents who had died in a boating accident when she was nine; as the indulged but disciplined orphan brought up by a maiden aunt; and finally, at her aunt's urging, as the bride of Clayton Rockford, the city's most handsome, rich, and eligible bachelor. He'd turned out to be nothing more than a wife-abusing, gambling drunk who had wed her for her money—and very nearly squandered it all, had some not been left in trust.

Fortunately Aunt Hannah had not lived to see the folly of her matchmaking. It would have broken her heart.

Mary leaned forward, folding her arms on the table.

Mary Smith.

It had turned out to be as good a name as any, plucked out of the air as she arrived in Whispering Bluff, Colorado, on Christmas Eve. She'd fainted in front of the post office, and Jane had taken her to the Hostettlers' ranch where the daughter, Becca, and their housekeeper, Helga, had delivered little Nancy.

Mary shook her head, remembering her pain and her dread and how Becca, the would-be doctor, and Helga, with five children of her own, had eased Mary's mind and calmed her fears and cared for her then and afterward with the most loving and tender hearts.

The family had called Nancy their personal Christmas baby. Good folks. They'd kept them both until Mary had found this place.

She could hardly believe it had been only three months ago.

Mary Smith, the name that would keep her safe—keep Nancy safe.

What did it matter that the good people of Whispering Bluff suspected her of being a "fallen woman"? She could tell by their furtive glances, interrupted conversations whenever she passed. Even Jacob Hostettler and Peter and Becca, even Jane. Even the pastor and his wife were not sure. She could see it in their kind, forgiving eyes.

But she didn't mind. No one here must know of her violent

past. Better they should think her a fallen woman than a felon.

Spotting her Bible between the cookbooks, she sighed and dropped her gaze.

She hadn't touched it since she'd placed it there. This soul-baring book, not opened since that awful night in December.

What troubled her the most and perhaps the reason she felt so alienated from the Almighty was her lack of remorse. She should feel guilty, be repentant. But she couldn't bring herself to be. She knew in her heart, faced with the same circumstances, she would do the same again.

The kettle began to whistle. She rose and carried the teapot to the stove—took the teapot to the boiling water—as her English aunt had instructed her.

Dear Auntie Hannah, perverse, punitive, but loving, who had done her best to teach the obstreperous orphan to be a lady, skilled in the womanly arts, and to appreciate the finer things in life. She knew she had been a challenge to the dear, long-suffering woman.

As the tea steeped, she leaned against the sideboard, gazing absently through the kitchen window, across the moonlit landscape, beyond the scattered trees to the house on the other side of the vacant lot, the last house on Mulberry Street before it curved onto the open road leading out of the small rural town.

In the dim moonlit night, the one-story cottage looked like a mutt on its haunches, the back porch its snout; ungainly, unattended, its blemishes of neglect hidden in the shadows.

The occupant, a terse, morose man with whom she'd hardly exchanged five words, was—which ever amazed her—the schoolmaster of Whispering Bluff. It was difficult to imagine how he could possibly relate to children. The indifference with which he treated his own small son was evidence enough. It broke her heart the way the poor little fellow followed his father around like a shadow, begging for attention.

She poured herself a cup of tea, added a tad of cream and a half teaspoon of sugar, stirring thoughtfully.

She had no inclination to be neighborly, that was for sure. Neither, obviously, did he. Which of course was all just as well, under the circumstances.

She lifted her cup and took a satisfying sip, savoring the fragrant hot brew as it warmed all the way down her throat.

She was about to lift the cup again when out of the corner of her eye a flash of white caught her attention.

two

Mary leaned forward.

It was the child next door, running down the back steps of his house. The schoolmaster's boy racing as fast as his short legs could pump! If he made it to the woods that led down to a swift-running creek, he could drown or be impossible to find.

A coyote's howl rent the night air.

Mary charged out the kitchen door and down the back steps, heedless of her bare feet and that she was clad only in a nightgown. She cut across the vacant plot between the two houses.

"Child! Little boy!"

He didn't acknowledge her cries or veer from his path.

Just as the branches of the dense thicket reached out to snatch him, she caught up and, grabbing a handful of his nightshirt, dragged him back.

The terror-stricken child turned in her grasp, and rather than try to run away, he locked his arms around her neck, clinging with a fierceness that nearly choked her.

She held his small, quaking body close, felt his wildly beating heart against her breast, the wash of his tears on her cheek.

"There, there, don't be afraid," she soothed, running her hand over his tousled curls. "You're all right. What frightened you? Was it a bad dream?"

She looked over at the dark, silent house and wondered at the secrets that had caused such fear in this small, innocent child.

Was it his father?

A crisp breeze whipped around them, and it was then she realized she was clad only in her flannel gown and her feet were bare.

She hadn't even noticed as she ran across the rutted ground, jagged with sharp twigs and stones. But now, as she gingerly minced her way back across the rough terrain, the few yards to the child's house seemed like miles. By the time she hobbled up the back steps of the schoolmaster's darkened cottage and pounded on the door, the stabbing pains in her icy feet were almost unbearable.

"Schoolmaster! Schoolmaster!"

After a long disturbing moment, a dim light appeared at a nearby window. She heard a shuffling behind the door and a drowsy male voice, thick with impatience. "Can't it wait until morning?"

"No!"

There was a moment of silence as if he were trying to make up his mind. The knob rattled, the hinges squealed as the door creaked open.

A large man in a dark dressing gown filled the threshold. The kerosene lamp he held cast the planes and shadows of his face in sharp contrast: broad forehead, deep-set eyes, a straight, prominent nose. A hard, uncompromising mouth!

He shifted the lamp, and the light poured over her and the child.

"Timmy!" he gasped.

With his free hand, he reached for the boy, and with a groan, he pulled the lad against him. The child turned, clinging to his father with the same fearful intensity with which he had clung to her.

Maybe it was the chill air or the wrenching ache of her feet, but she was not moved nor mollified by the man's obvious emotion. She was outraged by his carelessness!

"What kind of father are you? Don't you lock your doors? It's after four," she railed. "If I had been able to sleep, the Lord only knows what would have happened to him."

"I—" The schoolmaster started to speak.

"Unbelievable!" she muttered, shaking her head. She didn't

have time to listen to his excuses—her own child was alone.

"Thank you."

She paused.

"I'm very grateful." His voice was deep but with little inflection. "Sometimes Timmy walks in his sleep."

"All the more reason to lock your doors!" she said impatiently as she took her first agonizing steps down the stairs, holding tight to the rail.

But when her foot hit the cragged ground, a paralyzing spasm of pain shot up her leg. With an anguished moan, she clutched the rail and sagged to her knees.

"You're hurt!" The schoolmaster put down the boy and bounded down the stairs.

"Only when I try to walk," she muttered, gritting her teeth as she struggled to rise on raw, frigid feet.

He laid a detaining hand firmly on her shoulder, forcing her into a sitting position on the bottom step. "Don't move!" he commanded, placing the lamp next to her.

Before Mary had a chance to protest, he had disappeared into the house. He returned a moment later carrying a down comforter. It all happened with such dispatch. He had draped the comforter around her before she realized exactly what was happening.

Without so much as a "by your leave," he hoisted her up into his arms, carrying her as if she weighed no more than the coverlet in which she was wrapped, and strode after the child, who was now trotting ahead, holding the lamp.

"Are you insane? Put me down!" she commanded, struggling in his arms. "That poor little fellow's tender feet should be slashed to shreds worse than mine."

"Tough as leather. Those *tender* little feet see shoes only when he has to wear them to school." He tightened his grip. "Not like the pale porcelain feet of soigné ladies."

I don't need his sarcasm. All I did was try to save his child.

The boy hesitated at the bottom of her back steps.

"Go on up and open the door," his father commanded, following close behind.

"You can put me down now," Mary insisted when they reached the top. "I'll be fine."

But again he chose to ignore her as he pushed open the door onto the porch and entered the kitchen, setting her down on a ladder-back chair by the table.

The kitchen was filled with steam, the kettle hissing on the stove, nearly empty. He pushed it off the plate.

"Do you have—"

"Shh, you'll wake the baby."

"—some clean cloths and alcohol?" he whispered, his first move at conciliation.

"That won't be necessary." She pushed herself to her feet. "I'm quite capable of taking care of myself, thank you." She winced and fell back into the chair.

"So I see. It's the least I can do."

There was little use in arguing. Clearly he was not about to budge. Be it from guilt or compassion was hard to tell from his intractable expression.

She could just imagine the authority with which he controlled his students, the unyielding air. . .except, of course, for his bed-tossed dark hair.

She pulled the comforter more tightly around her. "You'll find everything you need in the cupboard above the sink."

Mary looked down at her injured feet. Scratched and bleeding, they were not a pretty sight. "There's soap on the kitchen counter," she murmured as he poured what remained of the hot water from the kettle into a large bowl then added some cold.

On the table beside her, he lined up all the things he would need to attend her wounds: the soap, the salve, the strips of torn rags. Silently he knelt in front of her and with surprisingly gentle hands lifted her feet into the soapy water.

She drew a sharp breath and pulled back, but he held her

ankle firmly. "I know it stings. I'm sorry. But we've got to get these lesions cleaned. You don't want them to get infected."

The boy moved closer, stood at his father's elbow, following every movement, transfixed, as she herself became transfixed, watching the man as he washed her feet, scraping out the most minute pieces of dirt and gravel with meticulous care. She studied the efficient movement of his lean fingers—ministering with almost a tenderness—as he bathed her feet in the soapy water, rinsed them in clear, stroked the salve on the bottom of each foot, and carefully tied the strips of rags around them.

He rose, and just as methodically as he had laid the items out, he returned them to their proper places.

"Very professional," she observed, considering him with piqued interest.

"Half the job of being a schoolmaster is ministering to the wounded. You should soak them in Epsom salts." He helped her stand. "Are the bandages too tight? Do you think you'll be able to manage?"

She took a tentative step, leaning on his arm. He steadied her as if she were a feather, studying her with fixed concentration. He was at least a head taller than she, with hair, albeit unruly at the moment, as black as hers and eyes dark and guarded, holding no hint of humor. "Will you be all right until morning?"

"It is morning," she said, glancing at the clock.

"So it is."

She watched his hand brush his son's head.

"I'll check in with you later."

She lifted her eyes. "That won't be necessary. I can manage from now on."

"Nevertheless, I'll check."

She shrugged and turned to the boy. "You mustn't scare us like that again, sweetheart."

Silently the child stared up at her. His dark eyes were intelligent, like his father's and just as guarded.

"He won't. Will you, Timmy?" The schoolmaster glanced at his son.

He picked up the lamp from the table where the boy had placed it and moved toward the back door, urging the child before him.

Mary leaned against the counter, watching their progress across the vacant lot toward the copse of mulberry trees that separated their two properties. A pale triangle of light bobbed in front of them, its apex high in the man's outstretched hand, his other on the child's shoulder, guiding him.

Protecting him.

There was something sad about the pair: the small child; the tall, broad-shouldered man, his movements brisk and focused, hurrying the boy toward the sanctuary of their house.

Silence separated them but held them tight in a cocoon of loneliness and isolation.

Two silhouettes against the pale line of light emerging along the horizon as the sun crept onto the plains.

three

"Morning, Miss Janie." White-haired Luke Thompson looked up from sweeping the boardwalk in front of Thompson's General Store, next door to the Whispering Bluff Post Office and Telephone Company.

"Morning, Mr. Thompson."

A brisk March breeze picked up the fringed corner of Jane McKee's sky blue wool cape and a wisp of her bouncy blond curls. She stepped onto the boardwalk.

The wiry little man leaned on his well-worn broom. "Or should I call you *Sheriff* Janie?"

Jane blushed. "*Jane* is just fine, Mr. Thompson. I'm not used to the title *sheriff* yet. It seems it still belongs to my daddy."

"Know what you mean. It was a sad day when he went. And so suddenlike." The man shook his head. "But you're goanna do fine! Just fine! With Deputy Spike as the brawn and you the brains, we all expect everything to go smooth as silk. Yep! Smooth as silk."

"Well, thank you for that vote of confidence, kind sir." Jane gave him a dimpled smile and deep curtsy.

"That's not to minimize your skills with the rifle," Luke Thompson said hastily. "No siree! Coming in first in the county competition over all those blowhards is not to be sneezed at." His blue eyes twinkled beneath their bush of white brows. "No siree! Not to be sneezed at! This town is in good hands with you, little lady. Absolutely! Real good hands."

"Well, thank you, Mr. Thompson. You always have been one of my biggest fans."

"I never doubted you'd be able to fill your papa's boots," he said, his gaze innocently scanning her denim-clad figure

21

down to her toes. "Although two of your daintily tooled boots would fit into one of his big clunkers, yours move a whole lot faster." The proprietor rested the broom against the frame of the store entry and absently finger-brushed on either side of the middle part of his thinning hair. "I loved your papa. You know that. But he—"

Jane interrupted. "I'll try my best to be a good sheriff. You can count on it." She didn't need to be reminded that her daddy was a lazy man and for the last few years she'd practically run the jail single-handed—not that it was all that big a job in a town the size of Whispering Bluff—but the town's folks knew it, and when he passed, it was just natural to vote her in. Still, she was honored they'd showed such confidence.

She stamped her feet to get the frozen mud off. "I'm hoping the buckskin I ordered for the new uniform I designed has arrived. If it has, I'll be in to purchase the lining from you. Denim is fine for every day, but for special occasions, like the Fourth of July parade and Whispering Bluff's other important celebrations, I think something more appropriate is called for. Don't you?"

Mr. Thompson smiled at her fondly. "Whatever you say, Miss Sheriff Janie. But in my opinion, you'd look appropriate in anything you put on."

"Isn't it the truth!" A round, stylish little lady, not much taller than Jane but with considerably more pounds per inch, stepped up onto the boardwalk. "With Janie's perfect little figure, she could make a flour sack look smart."

"It's my sewing skills." Jane grinned, whirling around. "Mavis, you sly one, sneaking up behind me. . ." She leaned over and gave her friend a peck on the cheek.

Mavis Dodd, the town seamstress, shrugged in mock exasperation. "I'm glad not everyone has your talent, or I couldn't make a living. You can sew, you can cook, you can shoot a gun. What can't you do, Jane McKee?"

"I can't seem to get a man." Jane laughed lightly, dropping

her arm around the waist of the plump, cherub-cheeked woman. "Morning, Henrietta," she called to the postmistress as the two entered the mail office.

The purse-lipped sourpuss glanced up with a perfunctory nod and returned to her conversation with Eunice Figg, the tall, rawboned mayor's wife. "That's disgusting! Not that I'm surprised. I always suspected she was *that* kind of a woman."

"Who's *that* kind of woman?" Mavis asked before Jane could give her a warning pinch.

Jane opposed encouraging gossip, as did Mavis. . .sort of. Mavis didn't spread it—except maybe to Jane—but she liked to listen to it.

"Tell them, Eunice," Henrietta said.

"You go ahead." The gangly woman in her new muskrat coat and matching cloche drew a long, self-conscious sniff into her beak of a nose.

"You're the one who heard it," Henrietta insisted.

Eunice Figg sighed as if she were about to make a great sacrifice. "You know I'm not one to gossip—"

Jane and Mavis exchanged skeptical glances.

"—but seeing as it involves the schoolmaster, I suppose you could say it affects the whole community." Her bony cheeks pinked. The small blue eyes closely flanking her nose glinted with anticipation.

"Well"—she leaned forward—"it seems Sara Beth Jones told Miss Lilly that Bertha Warner told her that Doc told her this morning at breakfast, that last night, somewhere around four thirty when he was coming back from the Simmons' farm—it seems old Sam was having another attack—"

"Gall bladder," interjected Hazel Pryce, who had poked her head in from the telephone office.

Postmistress Henrietta flashed her sister an impatient look. "Will you get to the point, Eunice!"

"Do you want to tell it, Henrietta?" Eunice Figg crossed her arms and glared at the woman behind the mail counter.

"No, no! You go on, dear," Henrietta, said sarcastically. "We've all got nothing but time."

Eunice arched a brow, sniffed, and continued. "Anyway, it seems Doc was trotting along in his buggy down Mulberry Street when he saw a light bobbing along in the vacant lot between the schoolmaster's house and that Mary Smith's place. Well, of course he was curious. . .as anyone would be. . . ." She lowered her voice. "He stopped his carriage, thinking perhaps somebody might need his help. What he saw. . ." She glanced around at her attentive audience.

They drew a collective breath.

"What he saw. . .was the schoolmaster carrying that woman, Mary Smith, across the vacant lot."

Mavis whispered, "How could he see if it was four thirty in the morning? It had to be too dark."

"That's the disgusting part!" Henrietta interjected.

"The schoolmaster's little boy was carrying the lamp for them." Eunice's breath whistled down her nose. "To make matters worse, if that is possible, the schoolmaster was wearing his night attire and that woman, Mary Smith, was wrapped in a *blanket*!"

"One wonders what she wore under it," Hazel mused. "If anything!"

"Nothing would surprise me about that woman, Mary Smith," Henrietta said. "But the schoolmaster—I never expected it of him."

"That's what I said when I told His Honor the mayor."

"You mean your husband," Mavis said.

Eunice Figg shot her a hard look.

Ever since Leonard Figg had been elected mayor, his wife no longer referred to him by his Christian name but by *His Honor the mayor*.

As if anyone could forget, with her airs.

"As a result," Eunice continued, "His Honor the mayor and members of the school board and the city council—at my suggestion—are going to pay the schoolmaster a visit this evening. It seems very apparent to me that he is not the kind of man we want influencing our children!"

"Given the incident only happened a few hours ago, don't you think that's a pretty quick leap to judgment?" Jane was so incensed by the vile insinuations she could hardly contain herself.

Mary Smith had become a close friend since she'd arrived on Christmas Eve three months ago and certainly had been the model of propriety. Jane had especially come to admire Mary for her sweet ways and independent spirit.

"The facts speak for themselves," Henrietta said primly.

"What facts? You don't have any facts! You only have fourth-hand what Doc Warner says he saw." Emboldened by anger, Jane took a deep breath. "I know Mary Smith. She is a sweet person who takes loving care of her baby and doesn't go around poking her nose into other people's business or gossiping about them! Besides, she's a married woman!"

Henrietta raised an eyebrow and gave Eunice Figg a pregnant look. "Is she now? Then why doesn't she get any letters from her husband? Or for that matter, post any to him?"

"And if she is married, why is she gallivanting around in the dead of night with the schoolmaster?" Hazel chimed in.

"Perhaps Jane's right. Perhaps we should withhold judgment," Eunice Figg said, suddenly appearing to take a more judicious approach. "Until we get all the facts." She sniffed. "Which we will soon enough when His Honor the mayor and the school board and city council visit the schoolmaster tonight."

Jane had heard enough! She didn't believe any of it. Not for a minute! Not about the quiet schoolmaster—from what little she knew of him—and certainly not about Mary.

Even though busybody Henrietta hadn't seen Mary post any letters to her husband. . .or receive any. . .*Mary has her reasons*, Jane thought staunchly, and they were no one's business but her own.

And small wonder Mary kept things to herself. Jane had seen the way people treated her, practically shunning her, and for no other reason than their vicious suspicions.

Jane's sense of fairness and justice loomed in front of her like a beacon on a stormy night.

This wasn't just harmless gossip these busybodies were up to! This was character assassination! And tonight *His Honor the mayor* would be leading a lynch mob.

Well, she was going to put a stop to it.

She swung around, her blue cape whirling, and headed for the door.

"Janie," Mavis called in surprise. "Where are you going?"

Henrietta pulled a box from beneath the counter and held it up. "There's a package here for you, Jane."

"Later!" Jane muttered through gritted teeth.

The last thing she heard, before the door swung closed, was Eunice Figg's rasping contralto. "Well! I wonder what set her off?"

Jane stomped across the boardwalk, her boots slapping the planks with the resolute cadence of anger and frustration.

They had their nerve!

That pretentious Eunice Figg, for all her airs, with that rascal son of hers, strutting around town like he owned the place just because his papa was "His Honor the mayor." Why, more than once, his antics, hankering after Billy Jean Johnson, had almost landed him in jail.

She could give the town an earful about that boy, all right. But of course she wouldn't. But she'd sure like to.

Distracted in her ire, Jane stepped off the boardwalk and came near to being hit by Angus Apple's buckboard.

"Better watch out where you're goin', Miss Janie," he called good-naturedly. "Wouldn't want to run over the sheriff afore she finished her first week."

"Wouldn't want that, either, Angus." She threw him a

chagrined smile and a perfunctory wave as she hopped up onto the porch in front of her office.

She stood for a moment, her hands on her hips, breathing hard.

Sara Beth Jones, Miss Lilly, and Bertha Warner, three of the worst gossips in town! You could only believe half of what they said and the other half was suspect.

And Henrietta—what a self-satisfied, know-it-all prude she was. And her sister, Hazel, was no better. Mean little mice, always sticking their twitching noses into other people's business. No telephone conversation in Whispering Bluff was private, no letter or package beyond their scrutiny.

I swear, I'd lay odds that Henrietta Pryce can read through steel.

Frustrated old maids living through other people's lives!

Jane stopped short and stared at her reflection in the window etched with the words SHERIFF'S OFFICE.

That was certainly the kettle calling the pot—or was it the pot calling the kettle?—well, black, anyway. Here she was talking about the spinsters Pryce. She didn't see any serious beau breaking down her own door. And she wasn't getting any younger, either.

She'd better button her thoughts. She was sounding as judgmental as they. Though at least she kept her thoughts to herself and didn't talk them all over town and spread malicious and unfounded gossip.

She pushed open the office door with a bang.

Spike Terrell, the bulky, dark-haired deputy dropped his feet off his desk with guilty haste and snapped closed the penny paperback he'd been reading.

"Catching up on big-city law enforcement?" Jane asked sarcastically, flinging off her cape and hanging it on the hook behind the door next to her holster and gun.

"Ya never know when the information might jest come in handy," he murmured, shoving the cheap tome into his bottom drawer.

Spike was addicted to lurid "true" crime stories that took place in Chicago or New York City and had covers with hands pointing pistols at scantily clad women.

Jane didn't approve. She believed that there wasn't enough time to read all the good books in this world, so why waste time reading bad ones? When he left them lying around and messing up the office and being a bad influence on their clients—the felons and drunks—she had no qualms about consigning them to the trash. She did, however, draw the line at foraging in his desk drawer.

She plopped down into her daddy's old leather chair and swung around to face the window.

Mavis was walking out of the post office now with Eunice Figg, chatting it up nice as you please. Jane knew she shouldn't, but she felt betrayed the way Mavis was smiling up at the larger woman, trading pleasantries. . .or worse, continuing to besmirch dear Mary's character.

Mavis was sweet but inclined to lean with the wind.

Mary's friendship was precious to Jane, and Jane would do anything to protect her.

Mary filled a void in Jane's life.

In the last few years, Jane's three closest friends since childhood—the four musketeers, they called themselves—had been separated, either by choice or circumstance.

First Isaac, barely seventeen, whose tyrant of a father, Jake August, in a fit of fury—no one ever knew what set him off—had thrown his son, along with Isaac's battered old guitar, into a boxcar on a train heading east.

Jane had gotten only one letter since. One letter from her cinnamon-haired, freckled friend, just to let her know he was still alive.

Much as she missed him, she knew his mama, Jackie Lee, missed him that much more. Sometimes when she saw the sad-faced woman, all broken from the abuse of that mean old husband of hers, it made Jane want to cry.

It would be better never to have a husband at all than one like Jake August. . .except that he had fathered Isaac.

A year after that, Becca had taken off for medical school, and even during her years attending college managed to marry Peter, the only young man Jane would have considered. And, married or not, Peter was working the ranch so hard he rarely took time to socialize anymore.

Jane had never felt so lonely.

Then Mary Smith rode into town, and Jane had gotten to know her and to love her. Nothing could convince Jane that this woman she had come to admire so much, with whom she had so much in common, had anything but the highest moral principles. Everything about Mary Smith bespoke of taste, quality and character, generosity and kindness.

It was the truth. Mary had filled a void. And since the new schoolmaster's arrival, Jane had even begun to feel a stirring in her heart. Then to have both of them involved in such unsavory gossip was more than she could accept.

Now, staring out the window at the post office across the street, Jane felt as agitated as a drop of water on a hot skillet, sitting there just ruminating on it all and doing nothing. Knowing that when Henrietta and Hazel got their turgid tongues a-wagging, rumors spread like wildfire in the small town.

And worse, a "posse" was being formed right at this very moment to meet with the hapless schoolmaster who, she was sure, was just as innocent as Mary.

Jane tapped her fingers nervously on the desk.

Mary was a very private person. The last thing Jane wanted was for her to think that she, Jane, was snooping or didn't trust her. But something had to be done. And fast! She had to find out the truth, clear Mary's good name before it was too late—to say nothing of that of the schoolmaster.

She whirled her chair around and poked the snoozing deputy. "I'll be gone a couple of hours, Spike." Slipping into her cape, she pulled open the door. "Stay alert."

four

The early spring sun slanted high by the time Mary finally made her way up the stairs, one painful step at a time. She was exhausted from the most perfunctory chores of preparing breakfast and tending to three-month-old Nancy. She dropped onto the bed, lifted her throbbing feet, and settled against the pillows to ruminate on the rewards of being a Good Samaritan as she absently patted the gurgling baby on the sun-dappled quilt beside her.

Her preoccupied gaze drifted out her bedroom window. Through the first leafing of the mulberry trees, she spied the schoolmaster's board and batten house, solitary on its unadorned plot. No plant or bush to relieve its harsh isolation. A sad reflection of its owner.

She remembered the unexpected shelter she'd felt in the man's arms, the strength of him. How long it had been since she'd felt so physically secure. She couldn't remember.

She stroked the feathery softness of Nancy's baby-fine hair, reflecting on the whirls of dark waves on the man's bent head, his lean, capable hands gently ministering to her wounded feet. She remembered, too, the haunting sadness she'd sensed in him, mirrored in the eyes of his child.

There was something mysterious and lonely about the pair—and oddly compelling. Their solitude touched a responding chord. Had it been a matter of choice? Or was it a necessity, as it was with her?

She wondered what they concealed behind their silence.

Surely the burden of their secrets could not hang as heavy as hers.

Clayton's accusing face swam before her.

Clayton, with his glacial stare and blunt-fingered hands so opposite of the schoolmaster's, hands without tenderness or mercy, capable only of inflicting pain. She ran her thumb down the fading scar on her cheek. The unremitting reminder of his savagery!

Who could have imagined?

When they'd met, he'd been all charm and graciousness, expansive, eloquent in his conversation and his compliments. Tall, fair-haired, handsome! Few women could resist him.

And he had chosen her.

Oh yes, indeed, she had been a willing accomplice. Was it a young girl's trusting naïveté? Her ignorance?

Or her arrogance! It surely said something about her own character that she could be so flattered as to have failed to notice the lack of substance behind his smooth talk and friendly facade.

Had it not been for Nancy's sake, she might be with him still.

Or dead! She shivered, shutting out the dark memories of her escape.

A brisk knock startled her from her morbid musing.

She sat upright, glanced at the clock on the highboy. Eleven thirty!

Already?

Almost lunchtime. Who would be visiting her at this hour? Who would visit her at any hour?

Except maybe. . .

"Yoo-hoo! Mary, are you there?"

Jane!

"Can I come in?"

"Of course, dear. The door is unlocked. I'm upstairs in the bedroom. Come on up."

To have the town sheriff as her best friend was hardly prudent under the circumstances. But how could she not? Jane McKee made it her business to be everybody's best friend.

And Mary had so few.

On the other hand, maybe it was a smart thing to have a sheriff in her corner. It was like hiding in plain sight.

"I brought us lunch."

Sunny as ever, her blond curls caught up in the latest style, Jane shed her cape as she bustled into the room. But she pulled up short when she caught sight of Mary's swaddled feet. "What happened to you?"

Mary grimaced, adjusting back against the pillows. "A mad dog chewed on my toes."

"Be serious!"

"Well, that's the way it feels. It's a long story."

"That's why I came, to hear long stories." Jane frowned. "What can I get you?"

"You can get me a clean diaper from the basket under Nancy's crib." She picked up her baby and held her, nose to nose. "I'm afraid I've quite neglected you, my darling."

Nancy giggled and kicked her little feet.

"She seems none the worse for wear," Jane observed, handing Mary a diaper and tickling Nancy's bare tummy. "Hello, sweet pea. Are you glad to see your auntie Jane? I can hardly wait until I get a pretty one just like you." She sighed wistfully, hitching herself up on the bed and settling against the bedpost at the foot. "So, Mary, I'm all ears."

As Mary changed Nancy's diaper, she began her chronicle of the night before, starting when she had awakened that hour before dawn.

Jane interrupted. "I hate it when I wake up like that. It's too late to go back to sleep and too early to get up."

"Well, I got up." Mary snapped the safety pin closed on Nancy's diaper and reached for the pink crocheted sweater lying next to the pillow. She pulled it over the baby's head, tugging in the tiny animated limbs as she described how she had seen the streak of white outside her kitchen window. "I realized it was the schoolmaster's little boy."

"Timmy," Jane interjected.

"I didn't think. I just ran out the door." Mary gave Nancy a quick kiss and cuddled her in the crook of her arm. "I was so relieved to catch him." She shuddered. "I remember standing out there at the edge of the woods holding his shivering little body in my arms. Then I realized it was not he shivering. There I was in my nightgown. With bare feet!"

"Good grief! No wonder they're shredded." Jane crossed her arms as if she were protecting herself against last night's chill. "What did you do?"

"What could I do? I carried the boy back to his house. . . *very* carefully!"

"I can imagine John Aubrey must have been frantic."

"So that's his name."

"You didn't know?" Jane looked at her quizzically. "You've been neighbors for almost three months."

"We've never really had occasion to talk." Mary shrugged. "I've always just thought of him as the schoolmaster. Anyway, he obviously wasn't awake! It took him forever to answer the door."

Jane's eyes widened.

Mary nodded. "It seems the boy walks in his sleep."

"I'm really surprised John wasn't more responsible. If he knew that, why didn't he lock his door?"

"Precisely! Think of what might have happened if I hadn't been awake and seen him."

"Men!" Jane shook her head. "They don't think about those things. Even schoolmasters." She played with the edge of the colorful Eight Point Star quilt. "What John Aubrey needs is a wife."

Her pensive look was not lost on Mary. "How well do you know him?"

"Not very." Jane's violet eyes twinkled. "But I wouldn't mind knowing him better. He just came to Whispering Bluff at the end of the last term. I do know, though, that his wife died not too long before he arrived."

That accounts for his aura of sadness.

Feeling a twinge of guilt, Mary said, "I'm afraid I wasn't very nice."

"What did you say to him?"

"I can't remember exactly. I was just so angry at his carelessness. And my feet hurt so much. And then I fell. . ."

"You fell?" Jane leaned forward.

"And before I knew it, he had wrapped me in a quilt and was carrying me home."

"Where was Timmy through all this?"

"He was leading the way with the lamp."

Jane frowned. "It must have been about four fifteen, four thirty by then."

"About. He—the schoolmaster—John Aubrey carried me into my kitchen and insisted on taking care of my poor feet right then and there. He said it was the least he could do."

"Which, of course, it was."

"I must say he was very thorough, very gentle. He said it was all in a day's work for a schoolmaster."

"I'm sure." Jane slid off the bed. "Still, I think Doc Warner should take a look. It would be awful if your feet got infected."

"I don't think that's necessary. If I soak them in Epsom salts, they'll be all right."

"Nevertheless!" Jane insisted.

Actually Mary was somewhat relieved that her friend was taking matters into her own hands and made no further objections when Jane headed briskly out of the room and down the stairs to the telephone in the hall.

She heard the click of the receiver being lifted from the box, and then there was a moment's pause.

"Hello, Hazel, Jane here. Can you get me Doc Warner? Mary Smith has been seriously injured. It seems—" Jane proceeded to expand the story, embellishing the event almost beyond Mary's recognition.

Mary leaned forward, her interest piqued when Jane lowered her voice.

"You might tell your sister, Henrietta, and Eunice Figg and Lilly. . ." Her tone, though low, was crisp and sarcastic, without its usual lilting quality.

There was silence. Then her voice, impatient, continued. "Well, now you know. I'll wait while you get Doc on the line."

What in the world was Jane up to?

Another waiting silence.

"Hello, Bertha, Jane here. I take it Doc isn't in his office. When he gets in, will you please send him out to Mary Smith's house? She was seriously injured last night—"

Mary winced. Not from the pain in her feet, but having to endure again Jane's gross exaggerations as she chronicled the happenings of the night before to the doctor's wife.

Holding Nancy in her arms, she scooted to the edge of the bed.

Jane was concluding in a voice barely audible—but cloyingly sweet. "I know it wasn't your intention, Bertha dear, but unfortunately your chance remarks about what Doc saw last night caused some erroneous conclusions. Frankly, they could have been quite damaging to some innocent folks' reputations." Jane cleared her throat. "In the future, you might want to be a tad more circumspect."

Mary felt sick inside. They'd been seen last night, the schoolmaster carrying her in a blanket, from his house to hers.

And now it appeared the whole town knew.

When Jane returned to the bedroom, the look of sunny satisfaction on her face fell short when she saw Mary sitting on the edge of the bed. "What's the matter?"

Mary's throat tightened. "You didn't come to share lunch. You came to satisfy your curiosity!"

five

"That hurts! That really hurts, Mary." Jane's eyes filled with tears. "That you could even, for a moment, think that I would be other than fiercely loyal to you breaks my heart." She pulled a lace-trimmed hankie from her plain denim sleeve and dabbed at her eyes. "Why I love you, Mary."

Who don't you love?

Immediately Mary was flooded with chagrin. Looking down at her bandaged feet, she clasped baby Nancy close, unable to meet Jane's gaze. Dear, sweet Jane. How could she, Mary, be so thankless, so unappreciative as to make light of her friend's loving heart?

She owed Jane an apology. A big one! But the injustice, the frustration made it hard for her to speak.

Quietly Jane said, "I didn't come here out of curiosity, Mary dear. I came here to find out what *really* happened. . .and to set the record straight." She walked over and covered Mary's hand with hers. "And I think I accomplished that," she said gently.

"I'm sorry," Mary whispered. Tears welled up in her eyes and clogged her throat. "I don't know what got into me. It's just so humiliating that people would think that I. . . It's so unfair. But I had no right to take it out on you."

"I don't blame you for a minute, precious. Who wouldn't be upset?"

"Will you forgive me?"

"All is forgotten."

Nancy began to wiggle and fret in Mary's arms. "I think she needs to be fed."

"While you nurse her, I'll get our picnic ready." Jane gently chucked Nancy under the chin. "Eat hearty, sweetie." Patting Mary's arm, she spun and headed out of the bedroom.

A modest peace slowly seeped back into Mary's spirit as she sank back into the pillows, her baby in her arms. Not "the peace that passeth all understanding." Far from that! A more shallow peace, but deep enough for the moment, the peace of friendship, true and secure. Surely she had that in Jane, she thought as she listened to her friend's sweet soprano drifting up from the kitchen as the dear girl sang one of Mary's old favorite hymns, "Rock of Ages."

A few minutes later, she heard her footfalls on the stairs and Jane poked her head through the bedroom door.

Leaning over the crib, Mary glanced up. "Shh," she whispered, tucking the pink blanket around the sleeping Nancy.

Jane smiled and ducked out of the doorway as Mary slipped into the red silk kimono lying at the foot of the bed then padded down the stairs in a slow, painful path to the kitchen. She dropped into the seat she had occupied the night before and propped her feet on the chair opposite.

Jane had brought her own hand-embroidered cloth with matching napkins and her white Limoges china with the embossed design and laid it all out on the round oak table.

"If I'd realized how elegant this party was going to be, I would have dressed for the occasion," Mary pronounced with a smile, flipping back her night braid.

Watching Jane spoon mounds of chicken salad beside the triangle-shaped bread and butter sandwiches and slices of pickled peaches artistically arranged on the china, she observed, "Pretty fancy for the kitchen."

"Why not?" Jane placed a plate before each of them. "I believe in enjoying the things I love." She poured tea into fragile hand-painted cups. "I inherited these from Becca's mother, Faith."

"Mmm." Mary ran her finger lightly over the rim of the

saucer, remembering the treasures she had loved that were lost to her now. The treasures of her family that she could not—dared not—claim. It was true that old Mrs. Armitage had left fine things in this house when she died. But they held no memories for Mary.

"And for dessert." With a flourish, Jane produced from the basket a platter.

"Your famous chocolate cookies," Mary declared, smiling. "The best!"

Jane's pleasure shone in her sparkling violet eyes as she dropped down into a chair across the table from Mary. She swept her napkin into her lap and reached for her friend's hand. "Do you want to say the blessing, Mary, or shall I?"

Mary's throat tightened. She could feel the tension rise inside her. She glanced over at the row of cookbooks where her Bible hid. "You say it, Jane."

They bowed their heads.

In her sweet, lilting voice, Jane began. "Dear Lord, help us to live fearless and free, secure in the knowledge of Your good intentions for our lives. May we understand there are no limits to what You can envision and we can attain. And in so doing, Lord, make us as mindful of the needs of others as we are of our own." Briskly she added, "Bless this food to our use and us to Thy service. Amen."

Mary choked out an echoing "Amen" as Jane squeezed then released her hand.

Jane had gone to so much loving effort in preparing this delicious repast; Mary knew the least she could do to show her appreciation was to enjoy it. And she tried. She did! But it stuck like sawdust in her throat. Finally she could pretend no longer. She put down her fork. "All right, Jane, who was it who started the rumor?"

Jane glanced up in midbite. "Oh. . .well. . ." She finished chewing, swallowed, took a sip of tea, daintily dabbed her lips, and looked decidedly uncomfortable.

"I'm waiting, dear."

"It was really rather innocent," Jane replied, trying to sound offhand. "A chance remark by Doc Warner to Bertha this morning. It seems he was driving back from the Simmonses' and saw a light and. . ." She frowned down at her plate, obviously not knowing how to go on. "I doubt he drew the same conclusions as his wife did. You know Bertha."

"No, I don't."

"She exaggerates everything. Nobody pays any attention to her."

Mary crossed her kimono-sleeved arms. "Obviously some people do, or you wouldn't have felt you had to go to so much trouble to 'set the record straight'."

"They're not bad folks, Mary. It's just that Whispering Bluff is such a small town, and they don't have much to keep them interested."

"Except other people's business."

"They don't mean any harm."

"Ha!"

Jane shook her head sadly, bouncing the feathering of blond ringlets around her pretty face. "They don't know you, Mary. You kind of keep to yourself." She leaned forward. "Maybe if you socialized more. . ."

"Under the circumstances, that's the last thing I'd want to do."

"You're a mystery to them. And what folks don't know, they're suspicious of." Jane propped her elbows on the table and rested her chin on her clasped hands. "I wish they could know you like I do: the absolutely perfect mother, the sweet friend. . ." She smiled. "The Good Samaritan."

"You know the old adage: Good deeds never go un-punished." Mary made a face and glanced down at her feet. "I guess you could call me a prime example."

"Not just with Timmy. But I've seen you from my office window, when you take the time to chat with Davy

Thompson. You don't ignore him, like he's an embarrassment. You talk to him the same as you would to any other boy, not... well, you know, not like he's feebleminded."

"In this town, I have to make my friends where I can find them," Mary commented drily.

"And the way you don't draw away from Maude Walker and her ragged young ones but treat them all with respect and kindness, even though most folks won't let their children play with them because their daddy's the town drunk."

"Maybe because I know how it feels to be shunned."

"That's the Mary I know."

"Thank you for not mentioning the Mary who takes out her frustration on a friend." She gave Jane a fond smile.

The clanging of the front doorbell interrupted.

"That must be Doc." Jane jumped to her feet.

Mary could hear their voices in the front hall, Jane's lilting greeting, Doc Warner's gravelly baritone.

Mary'd had cause to see him only twice after she'd birthed Nancy, but she'd always passed him with pleasant greetings the several times they'd met in town.

As he and Jane entered the kitchen, Jane began describing Mary's injury.

"Don't bother," Doc said, placing his black bag on one of the empty chairs. "Bertha has already filled me in." His grimace when he said it, his glance in Mary's direction told her he had an inkling of the pain his chance remarks had caused, and his regret.

Doc Warner, midsize and in his midseventies, had impressive muttonchop whiskers, a thick mustache, and kindly blue eyes beneath bristly gray brows.

"So, let's take a look." He commenced to unwind the bandages. "Very professionally wrapped," he observed.

Jane scurried over to retrieve the abandoned lengths of cloth as he examined Mary's feet and redressed her wounds.

"Some pretty deep gashes there, but in a couple of weeks,

you'll be good as new," he said, snapping his bag shut. "Soak 'em in Epsom salts three times a day, as you've begun doing, and use the ointment I've left. I'll check back in a few days to see how much you've improved."

He gave her a fatherly pat on the shoulder. "I think you'll live."

"Was there any doubt?" Mary smiled. "What do I owe you for this visit?"

"We'll settle up later."

"You're welcome to stay for lunch, you know," Jane said, following him to the front door.

"Rain check, Jane. I'm on my way back to old Mr. Simmons' place. But you might save some of those famous chocolate cookies if you have a mind to."

Mary could hear the front door open and Doc's voice from the porch. "Your friend could use more allies like you."

"Mary's a wonderful person. It wouldn't hurt for you to help spread the word, too," Jane responded before closing the door.

Mary fought back tears.

If only Jane knew.

Every time Jane said something nice, Mary felt more like a fraud. The weight of her transgression hung like a yoke around her neck. She knew she could never be rid of it; she would be shackled with it forever, but for Nancy's sake, she must move forward.

By the time Jane reappeared, Mary had regained her composure.

For the balance of lunch, Mary remained locked in quiet guilt as Jane continued the litany she'd begun before Doc Warner arrived, of Mary's virtues and high moral character, her multiple talents, finally concluding that the upcoming church bazaar would benefit from an exhibit of Mary's lovely watercolors.

To Mary's relief, an insistent howl from the bedroom above

interrupted the soliloquy. She hobbled up the stairs to attend her baby's needs while Jane cleared up the dishes.

Nancy changed and fed, Mary returned to the kitchen to find Jane had brewed another pot of tea. As the afternoon sun melted into dusk, casting slanting beams of gold across the oak table, they sipped their final cup while Mary rocked the cooing, contented baby in her arms.

"Now that Nancy's a little older, you'll be able to attend church more often," Jane observed, spooning a bit of sugar into her cup.

Mary didn't remind her that the last time—the only time—she'd attended Whispering Bluff's Good Shepherd Community Church was when Nancy was christened, over two months before.

Jane crossed her arms on the table. "It must be awfully hard being a lone woman with a baby in a completely strange place."

Mary shrugged.

"I know you don't have family but what about your husband's? I'd thought you would have gone to them when the army sent him overseas."

"My husband was estranged from his family. I doubt they would have welcomed me."

True enough!

"But Whispering Bluff. . . Why did you choose Whispering Bluff, Colorado, of all places? Not that I'm not grateful," Jane added hastily. "But it's so out of the way."

"I don't know." Mary shrugged again. "When he left for service in the Philippines, I closed my eyes and this is where my finger landed on the map. And. . ." She thought fast. "I was carrying Nancy. I wanted to find a place that would be good to bring up a child if. . .if anything happened to my husband and I was alone. Some place with good solid values and clean air. Where better than a small, rural town?"

"It sounds like you came from a large, coal-dusted city,"

Jane concluded, gazing at her warmly. "I'm glad you chose Whispering Bluff. Give us time, Mary. You won't be sorry."

It was at that moment there was a brisk knock on the porch screen door.

six

Looking out the kitchen window, Jane whispered, "It's John Aubrey and his boy."

Mary saw the color rise in her friend's cheeks as Jane jumped to her feet, tore off her apron, and quickly tucked it into the picnic basket.

My, my, even the mere sight of the schoolmaster turns her aflutter. I had no idea the wind blew so strongly in that direction.

Mary tried not to smile too broadly as Jane fluffed her curls, smoothed her blue denim skirt with nervous, birdlike gestures, and leaned over to adjust the eyelet ruffle at her hem.

"I'll answer it," Jane said, her voice breathless. "You just sit right there."

As if Mary were going to fly to the door on winged feet. She chuckled. If anyone could squeeze a smile from her taciturn neighbor, it would surely be sunny Jane.

She watched Jane flit out to the porch and pull open the screen door. "John Aubrey. I fancy you're here to see our patient. Come in." Stepping aside to let him and Timmy enter, she gave him a shy smile. "You'll be happy to know Doc Warner says she will live."

"I'm glad to hear that."

Timmy stood behind him on the threshold, barefoot and in coveralls, while the schoolmaster was suitably attired for his profession in black, with a stiff collar and string tie.

Jane smiled down at the boy. "Hello, Timmy."

He didn't meet her eyes but affixed his gaze to his feet. He was clenching a bouquet of wilting wildflowers, the first of spring, so tight it seemed their stems might snap.

"Did you know Miss Jane's our new sheriff?" Mary asked

from where she sat at the table. "She's Sheriff Jane. What do you think of that? A lady sheriff."

Jane smiled. "I bet you'd make a good deputy one day, Timmy." After a beat of silence, she cleared her throat. "What beautiful flowers. I suppose you brought them for Miss Mary."

The boy moved back against his father, his gaze averted.

Jane glanced up at the schoolmaster.

He shrugged. "My little man of few words," he said, touching the boy's shoulder.

It doesn't help the child's shyness to make excuses for him, Mary thought.

"He picked the flowers himself," the schoolmaster said, giving his son an encouraging shove in Mary's direction.

Painful to watch! And his father certainly wasn't helping matters. One would think someone who dealt with children would know better.

Obediently the boy shuffled forward, stiff and awkward as a marionette. When he reached Mary, he thrust out his hand holding the bouquet.

"They're lovely, Timmy. Thank you." Shifting Nancy from one arm to the other, she took the straggly blooms and handed them to Jane. "Will you please find one of my finest crystal vases, dear?"

When she turned back, she was mildly surprised to find the boy still standing there. Somehow she'd expected him to skitter back to his father. Instead, she found his eyes fixed on her—sad, timorous brown eyes, liquid with longing.

Her heart lurched. The instinct at that moment to enfold him in her arms was overwhelming, and she might very well have had Nancy not already occupied them.

Tentatively she reached for the small hand now hanging limp at his side, and to her relief, he allowed her to take it. It was such a frail little hand, so delicate, like a captured bird whose bones would snap if she squeezed too hard.

She was even more astonished as he suddenly drew closer,

melted into her, really. When he withdrew his hand, she expected him to move away, but instead, he studied her face, running his fingers lightly over her lids, down her nose, over her cheekbones, and along her lips as if he were trying to memorize every angle by touch as well as sight.

She became aware of the silence in the kitchen and then Jane's renewed cheerful chatter as she arranged the flowers, commenting to the extreme on their beauty and fragrance.

"I'll bet you picked them down by the stream. Am I right?" Jane said, not waiting for a response.

Mary covered Timmy's hand and guided it to Nancy. "See how she grabs your finger? She has a tight grip, doesn't she?"

A small smile lifted the corners of his mouth.

She could have wept. He was such a beautiful child. "I think she likes you very much. She doesn't want to let you go."

She had an uncanny feeling, as if she were wrapped in the silent cocoon of this child's making. It was just the two of them, and for that moment, no one else really existed. . .until she suddenly felt the weight of John Aubrey's watching and glanced up.

For one dark, trembling moment she felt the heat of his focus, not at her but into her, divining the secrets that she'd taken such pains to hide. As if, without knowing, he somehow knew.

She shuddered and looked away.

"My goodness," Jane said, "what kind of hostess am I? Won't you join us for a cup of tea, John Aubrey?"

"No thank you. We just stopped by to check on our neighbor."

"And to bring me flowers," Mary whispered to Timmy.

"But it appears she's well taken care of." His voice was as impassive as the expression on his handsome face.

He wasn't about to let anyone see behind *his* dark facade.

He reached for his son's hand. "Good-bye, then." At the door, he turned back to Mary. "If you need anything, I'm just across the way." Nodding to Jane, he and the boy were gone. All that was left was the sound of their footfalls on the back steps.

For several minutes, their presence haunted the room, the silence interrupted only by the persistent ticking of the grandfather clock in the hall.

"He's a very unusual man," Jane mused, watching them through the kitchen window, as Mary had done at dawn. "So handsome." She turned. "But that child. He makes one want to weep. And only four years old."

Mary sighed. "Can you imagine, being that age with no mother, and a father who seems so. . .so detached? How did his wife die?"

"I don't know. An accident. That's all he'll say. He changes the subject if someone tries to talk about it." Jane shook her head. "It's all so sad. Such a tragedy." She continued gazing out the window. "Someday he'll find someone to love him and that dear child."

Mary caught a note of wistfulness in her friend's voice.

❧

John followed Timmy across the vacant lot, through the lengthening shadows of the mulberry trees. He glanced back and saw Jane at the kitchen window.

But she wasn't the one who filled his thoughts.

The feelings that had washed over him at the sight of Timmy leaning toward Mary Smith, like a thirsty plant lifting its face to the rain, had caught him quite by surprise.

He reached out and took his son's hand. "I think she liked the flowers, Timmy."

The boy nodded.

Oh how he wished he could give the child more. How he wished he could reach out, embrace him the way that woman, Mary Smith, had done. The way Joanna used to.

But even the simplest human gestures seemed almost beyond his capacity. And when he tried, he felt unnatural, like an automaton going through the motions of being a father. Doing his duty.

Why must he be so shackled by his own guilt and grief that any show of emotion seemed more than he could manage?

"Are you hungry?" he asked as he pushed open the back door. "Maybe we could have some of that leftover stew Mrs. Grice made yesterday."

Timmy nodded and sat down at the kitchen table.

John pulled the pot of stew from the icebox and a couple of plates from the cupboard and set them on the counter. "Mrs. Grice takes good care of us, doesn't she? She's a good cook and a good housekeeper. We're lucky to have her." He glanced back at the boy. "Which do you want, milk or lemonade?"

Timmy nodded.

"Well, which is it?" John sighed, opened the icebox again and pulled out the pitcher and held it up.

Timmy shook his head.

"Milk it is." He replaced the pitcher and pulled out a bottle of milk, fighting down a feeling of impatience. He had no right. If *he* couldn't cope with the horror they'd lived through, how did he expect a four-year-old to? It had been eight months now, eight months since. . .

In time Timmy would speak again.

He stoked the fire in the stove with some slivers of kindling then put the pot of stew on top.

Someday. . . Until that day, it was hard.

Pulling a glass from the cupboard, he poured milk into it and returned the bottle to the icebox.

Why shouldn't it be hard? It was no less than he deserved. His penance. But why need the child continue to suffer?

He set the drink in front of Timmy and sat down, waiting for the stew to heat.

He cocked his elbows on the table and wearily covered his face with his hands.

After the opening of his first play in one of Chicago's re-spected regional theaters, "Promising Young Poet/Playwright" had been affixed to his name.

Modest play! Grand ambitions!

But his job managing his father-in-law's leather goods factory had not given him time to pursue those ambitions. For that reason, at a sacrifice to everyone other than himself, he'd accepted the position of schoolmaster in Whispering Bluff, so he could earn a living and still have time to "follow his muse."

His muse! Pretentious fool that he was!

What did it matter if sweet, timid little Joanna would be separated from her family and everyone she held dear? It was his "muse" that was important.

The memory of that last night of her life was branded on his heart by the fire that doomed her.

Abruptly he stood up and paced to the window. He could see the lamp still burning in the kitchen across the way. He flattened his hands on the counter, stiff-armed, his head dropping beneath his hunched shoulders.

He looked out at the darkened landscape.

It was at just about this time of evening when they'd stopped to set up camp just outside Denver. He and Timmy were in a grove of aspens at the bottom of the hill watering the horse, Joanna above, setting up for supper.

He remembered the sound of the brook, the rustling of aspen leaves, and thinking what a lucky man he was. He had it all: a young wife who loved him so much she was willing to sacrifice everything for his happiness, a healthy young son who adored him, and he, himself, on the threshold of fulfilling his lifelong dream.

Then he heard the screams.

He turned and looked up just as the explosion of flames lit the evening sky. He remembered scrambling up the hill, frantic to reach her, clawing at the sodden earth, on his knees as much as on his feet; for every step ahead, he seemed to fall back two, his legs leaden, his heart pounding, his lungs bursting.

Too late!

She ran toward him, a moving torch, her arms outstretched. And then suddenly, from the fire's vortex, she seemed to spin up into the heavens.

What he remembered then was Timmy's unrelenting screams.

seven

Next morning Jane orchestrated casseroles from the ladies of Good Shepherd Community Church. "And I've hired you a housekeeper once a week: Mrs. Meade. I know you can afford it."

When Mary demurred, her friend turned up her pretty nose. "I'll hear no argument, Mary dear. Your job is to care for Nancy and get well. And there's no way you can do it without help. You mustn't be too proud to accept it."

As a result, within two weeks, Mary was quite herself again and, thanks to Jane, had made several new friends.

Of course there was the schoolmaster. But he could hardly be called a friend, even if he and Timmy did make regular, perfunctory visits to check on her progress. More, she surmised, out of guilt, seeing as how they were the ones who'd caused the problem, than out of any feeling for her personally. She had noticed, however, that Timmy did seem to be more responsive with each visit. Though not the same could be said of his father.

It occurred to her that perhaps some folks said the same of her. Jane had been right when she said the people of Whispering Bluff did not know her. And if she were to be honest, she'd had no one to blame but herself.

What folks had seen was a woman who swept into town in her fancy phaeton, her nose in the air, wearing elaborate clothes and purchasing one of the most expensive houses in Whispering Bluff. A woman, who kept to herself, was proud and aloof.

So what if it was all a charade? That she was driven by fear and guilt? That she lived looking over her shoulder? That the only place she felt safe was in her own house, and even then, not completely? That she jumped at every strange sound and slept better at dawn?

What mattered to them was what they saw. And first impressions were hard to alter. But alter them, she must! If she intended to live in this town, make it her home, raise Nancy here, their impressions would have to change.

She would have to change!

Not just on the outside but inside. And that was the hardest part of all.

She stepped out onto the back porch and looked past the paddock to the small stable where Hitch Chapell had hitched Queenie up to the buckboard for their trip into town when Nancy woke from her morning nap.

The bandy-legged old caretaker waved. "Ready when you are, Miss Mary."

She waved back.

If anything could wake her sleeping baby, it was the foghorn blast of Hitch Chapell's voice.

Leather-skinned, wiry, a man of few words, he had crinkly blue eyes and a walrus mustache browned from years of spitting tobacco.

To Mary he seemed as much a part of the place as the shrubs flanking the back door. Making him, she realized, a friend, as well.

During her convalescence the two had pored over pictures and catalogs and, of course, *The Old Farmer's Almanac*, choosing which vegetables and flowers to plant, and had purchased the seed packets through Burpee's catalog.

An insistent squeal from Nancy told Mary that Hitch's voice had done the trick. In short order, she had the baby clad in the pink sweater and matching cap that Mary, herself, had knitted.

Tying the bow beneath her daughter's dimpled chin, she smiled, grateful that her baby girl favored her with her violet eyes and dark, curling hair.

As she secured her own plumed velvet bonnet with a hat pin and pulled on her kid gloves, she glanced at the fine dresses lined neatly in the carved armoire—the expensively elegant dresses that had come between her and the ladies of Whispering Bluff. She shook her head. With her new resolve to become part of the community, she'd have little use for them in the future.

What would she do with them?

Pack them away, she guessed. Maybe someday Nancy would want them for dress-up.

She picked up her baby and hugged her.

And Nancy would ask all about the fancy teas and elegant parties where Mommy had worn the pretty dresses, and Mary would invent stories that would make her laugh.

Their first stop in town was Mavis Dodd's Couture and Chapeaus where Mavis took her measurements, and together she and Mary chose the fabric for three suitable summer frocks: a red and white gingham and a striped green poplin for everyday, and for church, a floral lawn print—assuming Mary had the courage to return to church.

Her next stop was the cobbler's, to be fitted for a pair of sensible everyday shoes.

And then, their final stop before heading home, to see if the package of seeds had arrived, and then one more: the distasteful act of performing a bit of necessary subterfuge.

Leaving Nancy in Hitch's gnarled, capable hands, she entered the Whispering Bluff Post Office and Telephone Company.

"Good morning, Miss Pryce."

Covered in her serviceable blue-striped, full-length apron, the dour postmistress gave a perfunctory nod without cracking a smile.

"Will you kindly post this for me?" Mary handed her a long, thin envelope addressed to Col. Clayton Smith, conveniently stationed far away in the Philippines with a battalion she had read about in the *Weekly Post*.

Henrietta took the letter, examined the address, and turned it over. "You forgot the return," she announced, handing it back.

Mary's heart sank. "Oh, I see I did," she stammered, caught in her own fabrication. "Do—do you have a pen?"

A disgruntled Henrietta slid her own pen and inkwell across the counter. "Don't make a mess. Some folks do, you know."

Mary scribbled her name and address on the back of the envelope in the poorest penmanship she could muster and slid the writing accoutrements back across the counter.

The postmistress examined Mary's scrawl then glanced over her half-glasses and shook her head. "Good luck if they need to return it." But to Mary's relief, she wasn't about to waste any more time on this nonsense.

By that time, Mary was so flustered she almost forgot the other reason she had come until Henrietta muttered, "Your seeds have arrived," and slapped an oblong box marked BURPEE'S on the counter.

Mary was beside herself with excitement.

Arriving home, she hurried into the house. Then, as soon as she got Nancy fed and down for her afternoon nap, she brought out the wooden flats stacked on the back porch that Hitch had constructed and filled with dirt. All afternoon she planted the little seeds, sticking the empty packets on a stick at the end of the appropriate rows, then placing the flats on shelves Hitch had made for that purpose in a warm, sunny spot in the kitchen where she could tend them and watch them sprout and grow.

In the meantime, this city girl, who'd never gotten her fingernails dirty before, began working side by side with Hitch, moving stones and tilling the newly thawed soil in preparation for planting her garden.

By the third week of April, the plants were large enough to put into the ground.

While Hitch grunted over the vegetable garden, Mary deposited her sleeping infant beneath the still-leafless oak.

Then with spade in hand, she squatted down and began digging the shallow holes into which she placed the small, tender flower plants, spreading them in random groups and colors like she'd seen pictured in the English gardens. As she planted, her excitement grew, anticipating the surprises when the plants matured and the buds popped open into bright blooms.

She loved the feel of the soil, the rich, loamy smell of it, the warm sun, the soft, caressing breeze.

Shadows lengthened without her notice.

Leaning back on her heels, she closed her eyes, listening to the rustling leaves and the birds chirping in the mulberry trees, the squawking of an angry jay, the mewing contentment of her baby.

"This is the day which the Lord hath made; we will rejoice and be glad in it."

It bubbled up inside her, the truth of it.

The reality of it!

She realized that for these precious hours, she had felt at one with the world and had been truly, truly happy for the first time since she could remember—and at peace.

That evening, with Nancy tucked safely in for the night, Mary sat alone at the kitchen table, her hands clasped in front of her, pondering the day—until what had been nagging her for months refused to leave her alone.

Slowly she rose and crossed the room.

She hadn't hidden it exactly. More ignored it. But there it was, peeking out from between her mother's *Fannie Farmer Cook Book* and *Miss Parloa's New Cook Book and Marketing Guide*, its worn spine shimmering with the gold letters, HOLY BIBLE, as if a beam from heaven were suddenly striking it—as if it were shouting at her!

She pulled it from the shelf and returned to the table.

For several moments, she stared down, seeking the courage to open it, wondering where to begin.

All these months she'd ignored God.

Well, not really ignored Him, although she'd tried mightily. But despite her best attempts, He had continued to be a nagging presence.

And today, in His most subtle, amazing way, at a most unexpected moment, the Lord had broken through her defenses.

She closed her eyes and, with a small prayer, let the pages fall open.

Jeremiah!

Why Jeremiah, of all books? Not one with which she was all that familiar. Certainly not one she would have chosen. Psalms, maybe, even the Proverbs. . .or the New Testament. But Jeremiah?

Her gaze fell to the bottom of the page.

"For I know the thoughts that I think toward you, saith the LORD, thoughts of peace, and not of evil, to give you an expected end. Then shall ye call upon me, and ye shall go and pray unto me, and I will hearken unto you."

Mary closed her eyes. She felt the tears streaming down her cheeks.

After all she'd done. After all the time she had suffered the guilt that she might be a murderess and an almost greater fear that she wasn't, that Clayton would still find her and Nancy, and even as she had continued to deny Him, He had remained steadfast. Waiting for her, her source of strength, peace. . .redemption.

But could it really be that simple?

eight

That night Mary slept without a single disturbing dream and woke refreshed, welcoming the day. She hummed happily to herself as she dressed and made breakfast, fed and bathed little Nancy. If there still remained a shadow on her joy, she thrust it to the farthest reaches of her mind and locked it there...at least for now.

In the weeks that followed, her garden drew her like a magnet. While the dew still sparkled on the leaves, she would squat down and let Nancy touch the damp buds, pointing to the burgeoning pansies, snapdragons, and petunias, with the promise of marigold and zinnia blossoms.

She had Hitch build a trellis by the back door where sweet peas lifted their heads in a cornucopia of color and perfume. Rosebushes planted by Mrs. Armitage bloomed in a glorious profusion of pink, intertwined the picket fence in front, and covered the arbor over the gate.

She saw in her garden a metaphor for her own renewal: from the darkness, to the sprouting seed of acknowledgment, to the bloom of redemption.

One afternoon as she tended the flowers along the side of the cottage facing the schoolmaster's house, she glanced up to see Timmy Aubrey standing nearby, watching her with fixed concentration. She was startled to see him but not surprised at his interest. Judging from the stark appearance across the tree-sprinkled lot, a lovely garden must be very compelling to a child.

"Hello, Timmy."

He hesitated then shuffled over and squatted down beside her.

"I'm pulling weeds. They're easy to pull when they're small like this. Do you want to try?"

She showed him how to avoid the small plants, and he quickly caught on. For a four-year-old, he was dexterous and certainly diligent as he worked by her side down the rows of flowers.

"See all those little buds? I wouldn't be surprised if some of them popped open by tomorrow. You'll have to come and check." She leaned down to smell them, urging him to do the same. "Look, there's a worm. I used to think worms were bad, like snails, but now they're my friends because they're so good for the soil. I read that in a book."

She turned and smiled at him. "They're also good for catching fish. But you probably already know that. Do you go fishing with your daddy?"

"On occasion," came a man's deep baritone from above her.

It was then she noticed the shadow cast across the lawn beside them.

The long, dark shadow of the schoolmaster!

She sighed inwardly. The man's morose presence was like a cloud blocking the sun.

Immediately she chided herself: Shame on her for her lack of charity, especially now that she knew the circumstances of his melancholy.

She looked up. He was wearing his usual black suit and brooding expression. "I hope you don't mind my borrowing your son."

"Not at all."

"He's a very good worker." Taking off her work gloves, she smiled at Timmy. "He and I were about to stop for a glass of lemonade. Won't you join us?" She stepped on the hem of her apron as she rose and stumbled forward.

John Aubrey reached out to steady her. "Your feet are still. . . ?"

"Oh heavens, no. They're quite fine. Just long skirts and

new muscles that I'm discovering." She laughed.

His hand lingered, as if he didn't quite believe her.

"Really," she said, smiling into his eyes. Hoping for a response.

As he withdrew his hand, his dark gaze swept her disheveled hair then lowered abruptly to her garden. "Lovely," he murmured, his expression alarmingly sad.

"Thank you." Bemused she removed her calico apron then leaned over to brush off the bits of dirt clinging to the hem of her dove gray cotton skirt. "It's not too late to start a garden, you know," she said, glancing at the stark outline of the house across the way. "Wouldn't you like to have one of your own, Timmy?"

The boy nodded soberly, then quickly glanced at his father for affirmation.

The man's response was quick and restive. "Perhaps next year." He glanced at Mary. "But I'm sure Miss Mary can always use a helper. Isn't that so?"

"By all means," Mary said, resting her hand on the boy's shoulder.

Shifting responsibility again, Mr. John Aubrey?

Had her lips moved?

The way he was eyeing her. . .

"We'll have our lemonade on the veranda," she said briskly. "You all go up and sit down. I'll be out in a minute. I just have to get Nancy up."

The man just didn't understand what a boy needed. . . or wasn't able, for whatever reason. . .or didn't want to be bothered. It was tragic!

With Nancy on her hip, she laid out the platter of oatmeal cookies and pulled the pitcher of lemonade she'd made that morning from the icebox. Her mind was detached, focused on the sad, small boy who seemed so emotionally crippled that it broke her heart.

Absently, she kissed Nancy while considering ways she

might engage this poor, love-deprived child without offending his father at the same time.

Then an idea popped into her head.

It was so obvious. Why hadn't she thought of it at once?

After checking her ordinary bun for any stray curls, she swept out onto the veranda and secured Nancy in the spooled-wood high chair beside the wrought iron table. "Will you men watch her while I get our cookies and lemonade? I think her stuffed bear is next to you in the swing, Timmy."

The child reached for the toy, slid down from his seat, and trotted eagerly over to Nancy. He tickled the furry bear against her nose. She reached for it, rewarding him with a dimpled grin.

"You are good with babies, Timmy. I'll know whom to call when I need someone to entertain Nancy," she said, glancing over her shoulder, her manner purposefully offhand as she hurried back into the house.

Returning she set the tray on the table and sat down in the peacock wicker chair behind it. Pouring the lemonade, she mused, "I was just thinking what to do with some of the seeds I had left over." She handed John Aubrey a glass and one to Timmy. "I know there were some radishes and onions. Green beans, I think. Oh, and corn. Yes, I'm sure there was corn. Help yourself to some cookies," she said absently.

"There's a spot near the back of the house large enough for a small vegetable garden, I think. I wish Hitch weren't so busy, or I'd ask him to help me."

Suddenly she smiled, as if a bright idea had suddenly been born. "Timmy! Would you be interested in helping me?"

The child's mouth dropped open in midsip. His large brown eyes lit with surprised delight. He nodded so vigorously that his small frame quaked and lemonade sloshed over the edge of the glass, leaving dark spots on his coveralls.

"Provided, of course, it's agreeable with your father." She looked askance at John Aubrey.

The schoolmaster stared back.

Oh-oh, was he taking her offer as an indictment?

Well, if the shoe fits. . .

After a pause, he said, "You're sure it won't be too much trouble."

Trouble, indeed!

Mary took a deep breath. "No trouble at all." She willed herself neither to let her relief nor irritation show. "In fact, I don't know if I'd even be able to do it without Timmy's help. Is tomorrow too soon to start?"

Timmy grinned.

For a moment, it almost seemed as if he were about to speak.

No such good fortune!

Mary broke off a piece of cookie and handed it to Nancy, who squished it between her fingers. "Then tomorrow it is. Right after you two come home from school."

Perhaps John Aubrey would offer his services, as well?

After a considerable pause and no response from the man, Mary, biting her tongue, passed another round of cookies.

"Excellent," John Aubrey said, helping himself. As did Timmy.

For the next few minutes, only munching interrupted the silence.

John Aubrey cleared his throat as if he were about to say something.

At last!

No. . .

Instead, he lifted his glass of lemonade and took a healthy swallow.

Mary had to admit, though, there was something gratifying about the way this widower and his son seemed to savor her modest culinary accomplishment: simple oatmeal cookies and fresh lemonade. She wondered how long it had been since they'd enjoyed such a repast, modest as it was, her being such a novice in the kitchen.

After a time, she said, "I suppose you two have been fishing at Rikum's Pond."

John Aubrey wiped his mouth with his napkin. "I understood it was on private land."

"The pond is. But according to Jane, the lowers, where it falls into the stream, is on public property."

"The sheriff should know, certainly."

Mary smiled. "She says it's the best trout fishing in the county. You like to fish, don't you, Timmy?"

The boy nodded.

"I'll bet if you asked Sheriff Jane she would be pleased to show you where the best place is."

He looked doubtful.

"And your daddy, too."

In fact, I think Jane would jump at the chance to take your daddy.

Mary smiled. "And you can show her where the best worms are."

Timmy rewarded her with a smile and leaned his head against his father's arm.

Another prolonged silence was just beginning to verge on awkward.

Finally Mary asked, "So, how long have you lived in Whispering Bluff?"

"Since the end of August, last."

When he didn't elaborate, she asked, "Are you happy here?"

Happy? That was not a very bright question. How could a man with such a perpetually cheerless expression possibly say he was happy?

John Aubrey set down his glass and shrugged. "It's fine. Takes time to settle in."

"I guess that's endemic to small towns," she said, feeling an irony of her own.

She followed his distracted gaze across the vacant lot to his house across the way.

A house. That's all it was, certainly not a home. And nothing about the property bespoke of any personal effort to make it one.

She felt a welling of impatience. Couldn't he see how important the comfort of a home was for his son's sake, if not his own? For a man who, according to Jane, purported to be so brilliant and talented, how little insight he had regarding the needs of the human heart. Especially those of a child like Timmy.

John Aubrey cleared his throat, the effort to make small talk showing in the crease of his brow. "What brought you to Whispering Bluff?" he asked, more out of politeness than interest, it seemed.

She glanced at Nancy. "For the same reasons as you, I suppose. I wanted a place that was safe and healthy for my baby."

"Yes. Well. . ." A shadow crossed his face.

"It was serendipitous, really. This was where I landed the day before Christmas. Nancy wasn't born yet."

He glanced at her ring finger. "And your husband?"

"My husband's in the military."

"I see."

"Nancy was born at the Hostettlers' place. They were so kind, taking me in the way they did. Jane was so kind. I expected the whole town would be."

Little did she know, then.

"I guess in the back of my mind I thought this was where I was meant to be. . .in case something happened to my—"

"Yes. . ."

There was an empathy in his gaze that caught her by surprise. Then, as if he'd betrayed a too personal side of his nature, he turned his attention to the glass in his hand.

"The Hostettlers called Nancy their Christmas child," Mary said.

"She's a beautiful baby," he murmured.

"Thank you."

"She favors you."

Mary felt her cheeks warm. *Did he mean that as a compliment?*

But when she glanced up, she saw his expression was as impassive as it had ever been.

Abruptly he rose. "Well, son, we don't want to overstay our welcome."

"Not at all," Mary said. But as she rose, she admitted to herself a weariness in the elusive company of this strange man. "Let me wrap up some cookies for you to take home with you."

"That's very nice. Thank you. Timmy can have them in his lunch tomorrow."

She watched, amused and impressed, as the small boy eagerly filled the napkin she'd laid out for the cookies and drew up the four corners, tying them in a neat knot.

She doubted there were many treats in that household. John Aubrey didn't impress her as the type to give much thought to what he ate.

She lifted Nancy from the high chair and followed them to the edge of the veranda.

At the top of the steps, John Aubrey turned.

"Thank you very much. It was. . .It was nice."

There was something in the way he said it, the haunted sadness in his eyes, that wrenched her heart.

"Thank you for coming, John."

She realized she had just used his Christian name.

He stood for a moment longer, studying her with an almost unconscious speculation that made her suddenly ill at ease. And then his expression changed, impassive once more as he looked down at the boy.

"Timmy thanks you, too, don't you, son?"

Timmy nodded solemnly, one little hand clutching his father's, the other, his precious cookies.

"Well. . .thank you again." John Aubrey turned and made his way with Timmy down the front steps of the cottage and across the yard toward that dreary house.

I hope he doesn't break Jane's heart.

nine

From his kitchen, John could see Mary Smith's immaculately groomed cottage through the trees. He'd stood there, watching as she cleared away the dishes from the veranda and now as her silhouette moved about her kitchen. The woman was almost Madonna-like in her grace and at the same time a loving mother hen—at least to his son.

Timmy climbed up on the chair beside the gateleg table under the window and peered out, following his father's gaze.

"You like her, don't you, son?"

The boy nodded, his eyes fixed on the house across the way.

"I reckon your garden will be in that open space between the oak and her back stairs. What do you think?"

Timmy pressed his nose against the glass.

Sometimes talking to the child was like talking to himself.

Although there was still a little sunlight outside, it was beginning to get dark in the kitchen. John picked a match from a metal box and lit the kerosene lamp in the middle of the table.

"You'll be five in just three weeks."

If Timmy heard, he didn't respond, still imagining himself across the way, it seemed.

"If you start your garden with Miss Mary tomorrow, and plant your seeds, by the time they begin to sprout, it will be May twenty-nineth. You know what that means." He paused. "Maybe if you tell her it's your birthday, she'll bake you a cake."

This time Timmy did turn and fixed his father with a narrow, unsmiling glare.

John sighed. "All right. So *I'll* tell her."

Now he gifted John with a smile.

Rarely did Timmy fail to read John's intentions. Silent he might be, but there was keen intelligence behind his son's liquid brown eyes. Four years old, and able to read the third-grade books, knew all his numbers, and did simple equations.

At first John had been concerned about taking Timmy to school with him. Wondering what he'd do to keep the boy occupied all day. But from the beginning, he had been amazed at Timmy's interest and concentration, and how much he had absorbed just from listening and observing the other children.

Timmy had always been advanced: his first words at eight months, full sentences by a year and a half. He'd been gifted in music, as well, blessed with perfect pitch, according to Joanna.

Although who'd know it now?

He got his musical talent from her. She'd always sung to him—even in the womb. That last Easter, just before they'd left for Colorado, Timmy and Joanna had sung a duet in church, "Jesus Loves Me," in two-part harmony. Just three years old then. Nobody could believe it.

He looked across at his son.

No songs now.

"We'll have to think of a way to celebrate," John said, studying the boy's profile: his slightly tilted nose, his pouty lower lip, and his pointy, dimpled chin. He might look like John, but he had Joanna's profile.

"Maybe by your fifth birthday you'll feel like talking again."

Timmy turned his face away.

"You're a smart boy, Timmy. There's so much in your head—"

Timmy swung around, his eyes as hard as jet beads.

"You could at least try—"

Abruptly he scrambled off the chair and without looking back ran from the room.

John stood immobile, listening to the swift patter of feet, the slam of a door.

The silence.

Sighing, he moved toward the hall.

He'd been through it before.

Gently he turned the knob and pushed open the door to the bedroom across from his own. He leaned against the jamb, sad and weary as he gazed down at the small body lying prone on the bed, face turned toward the wall.

No sobs. Timmy hadn't cried since Joanna died.

Even as he'd watched the horror, he hadn't cried. Only screamed, those dry, unrelenting screams that reverberated still in John's brain.

And her screams. . . Did Timmy still hear them, too? What was going on in his head right now, this minute, as he lay facing the wall?

John crossed the room and lowered himself down onto the edge of the bed. He felt his son's back grow ridged beneath his touch. As if John were an intruder.

Always it was the same.

"I didn't say you had to talk, Timmy."

Still, Timmy didn't move.

For several minutes, John sat there then stood up. "I'm going to warm our supper now—the meat loaf and mashed potatoes Mrs. Grice left for us." He waited. "Come out when you're ready."

What else could he do?

He felt helpless. Used up!

He felt. . . He didn't know what he felt—pity, sadness? Anger? Some of that, too.

Sometimes nothing at all!

That was the worst.

Back in the kitchen, his gaze drifted again to the cottage across the way, that place of warmth and life.

He knew what Mary Smith thought of him. He saw it in her eyes.

The truth was, she thought no less of him as a father than he thought of himself. He wanted to be different, more responsive. But how could one bring water from a well that had run dry?

He stoked up the fire and put the Dutch oven on the stove. He opened a jar of string beans and dumped them and the juice into a pot.

The woman, Mary Smith, seemed to know how to reach Timmy. Almost magically she drew him into her circle of warmth.

He looked across the yard.

She just might be the answer to his prayers. . .if he still believed in such things.

ten

Mary wasn't sure she had actually heard a knock at her back door the next afternoon. But when there was a second one, slightly less timid, she picked up Nancy and hustled down the stairs.

Timmy stood on the back steps, his small hand grasping a long, thin pole twice as tall as he.

"Ah, I see you've brought your own hoe, Timmy. Good thinking."

She glanced across the yard, hoping his father might have followed yet was not unduly surprised that he had not. Another lost opportunity to bond with his son. But what else should she expect?

Still, it made her sad.

"While I put on my sunbonnet, you run over to the stable and let Hitch know you're here. He's expecting you."

Mary sat in the shade of the oak on an old quilt she had laid out for Nancy and watched while good old Hitch put Timmy's little hands on the handle just in front of his and pushed with his own weight behind the small hand plow.

When they had tilled a plot about six feet by six feet, Hitch straightened, pushed back his stained cowboy hat, and wiped his brow and the back of his neck with a soiled red bandanna. "Yer on yer own from now on, partner."

Timmy looked quizzically at Mary.

Mary laughed. "Don't worry, Timmy, we're in this together." She scrambled to her feet, handed Nancy her favorite toy bunny, and picked up her own hoe as Timmy retrieved his.

With the little fellow watching and mimicking her every move, she showed him how to smooth out the tilled soil—

"Good job!"—and how to make the rows of furrows and spread the seeds.

"Now you cover them with a thin layer of earth. That's the idea. Perfect! You're a better farmer than I am."

By the time they had finished, they were both smudged with dirt and weary, and the sun was barely peeking over the tops of the mulberry trees.

"You are one fine worker, Timmy," Mary said, falling back onto the quilt. She patted the place beside her. The two rested side by side in silence, their eyes blinking up into the branches of the oak.

Covering Timmy's small hand with hers, she closed her eyes. The drowsy droning of bees in Hitch's nearby hives, the mixed perfume of fresh-turned earth and sweet peas from the trellis by the porch, the contented chortles of Nancy, dancing across the warm afternoon breeze, and the satisfying fatigue of honest labor sent her into that sweet, contented place where one floats between wakefulness and sleep.

At the crunch of footsteps, she opened her eyes and found herself looking up, not into the branches of the oak but into the solemn face of her neighbor.

John Aubrey stood above her, holding a pitcher of lemonade and two glasses.

"It occurred to me that hard workers could use some liquid refreshment."

"Indeed we can." Mary sat up. "That was my next order of business."

"It was the least I could do," he said, acknowledging her effort without actually saying thank you.

He poured a glass and handed it to Mary then another for his son. "I can't take full credit; Mrs. Grice was here today."

"I see."

"I didn't make these, either," he said, not breaking a smile as he brought out Mary's napkin from the day before, neatly washed and ironed. He spread it open, displaying four molasses cookies.

Timmy's hand shot out at once. A frown from his father reminded him to retract it as he turned imploring eyes on Mary.

"Such impeccable manners, Timmy. Clearly you have been well brought up." She glanced up at John Aubrey.

Still no smile.

Oh well, so much for frivolous banter. "Yes, thank you, I will try one." She brushed her hands on her apron and lifted a cookie daintily between two fingers. "Where's your glass? Aren't you joining us?" She moved nearer Nancy to make room for him between her and Timmy.

"I'm not staying. I have to go back and prepare a science project for school Monday."

Excuses, excuses! Still, Mary was a little surprised at her disappointment.

But who could blame him? she thought, suddenly aware that her sunbonnet was askew and her striped pinafore smudged— and heaven knew what else. "I must look a fright."

He frowned, giving her that familiar, assessing look of his, and then he did the strangest thing. . .for him.

He smiled.

What a nice smile he has, she thought, *gleaming white teeth, crinkly laugh lines around his dark eyes.*

"On the contrary, Mary Smith. You actually look quite fetching. Mud quite becomes you!" He turned to his son. "Don't you agree, Timmy?"

The child, chewing vigorously, nodded with equal enthusiasm.

"Besides, a woman with so kind a heart could not look otherwise." He made a slight bow and turned away. "Don't overstay your welcome, son," he shot over his shoulder as his long-legged strides ate up the distance between their two houses.

Oh my, Mary thought, looking at Timmy, bemused. *Was that a compliment?*

Even though Mary had warned Timmy it would be a week before there was even a hint of green, still, every day after school, he raced over and squatted down beside his vegetable garden, searching for sprouts.

Meanwhile, her own ornamental garden, in which he had become an avid weeder and snail collector, had exploded into a veritable bower of flowers, so profuse and beautiful as to attract a multitude of colorful butterflies and birds as well as the whole neighborhood. Trudy St. Cyr and her roomers from the boardinghouse on the corner often dropped by. Jane, Mavis Dodd, and Lizzy Molten, the barber's wife, made a habit of strolling through by way of the woods around noon, several days a week, and never went away without their arms laden with flowers. It seemed every bloom picked was replaced by three. So much so that on Sundays Good Shepherd Community Church was blessed with her blossoms on the altar. Perhaps she'd miscalculated just how many flowers she'd planted.

Clifton Walker even did a front-page feature in the *Weekly Post*: PARADISE IN WHISPERING BLUFF, with photographs of Mary's garden. In black-and-white, they hardly did it justice.

One afternoon Timmy came running over with a book illustrated by Kate Greenaway that he'd borrowed from the Whispering Bluff Library. He pulled Mary down on the grass and laid the book on his knees then opened it and pointed with excitement to the page:

> *Mary, Mary, quite contrary,*
> *How does your garden grow?*
> *With silver bells and cockle shells,*
> *And pretty maids all in a row?*

He looked up, his face wreathed in a proud smile.

"You can read that, Timmy?"

He nodded, closed the book, and placed it carefully on the grass beside him.

"That's amazing! And you're not yet five. And you found my name and another garden full of flowers. How wonderful!"

Moving closer, he threw his arms around her.

Her heart swelled with such a tender, poignant joy that tears threatened. *I mustn't cry! I mustn't!* She put her arms around him and rubbed her cheek against his soft curls.

She loved him. Dearly, wholly! She realized that she wasn't just being kindhearted, as his father had said. She truly loved him. He had enriched her life, brought her outside of herself and her concerns for her own and Nancy's well-being.

If she was a blessing to him, he was twice the blessing to her.

She glanced over at the neglected, unloved house across the way and saw John Aubrey standing by his back steps watching them, a dark, lonely figure in the afternoon sunshine.

For a long moment, they regarded each other across the abyss of his isolation. Then he turned, mounted the stairs, and disappeared into his house.

An isolation of his own making.

A gripping sadness claimed her thoughts, blessedly interrupted by the dissonant babble of female voices at her front gate.

Jane had warned her about this visit, something about a request. . .of which she would not divulge but gave Mary a teasing, secretive smile.

"I'm counting on you to be my courage," she whispered to Timmy, pulling him along beside her and squeezing his small hand as she peered around the corner of the house.

She stepped forward. "Good afternoon, ladies."

"Ah, Mary Smith, I'm glad we found you in." The velvet robin affixed to the silk yellow rose on the abundant garden atop Eunice Figg's jet-black hair bobbed as she spoke—as if searching out a worm in the woman's hat. "I think you know Bertha Warner. But perhaps you've not met our city hall secretary, Miss Lilly Johnson."

"Welcome." Mary smiled and inclined her head.

Bertha Warner straightened the wide brim of an immense mixed silk bouquet flattening the fringe of gray curls along her brow. "We've been admiring your garden."

"Indeed," Miss Lilly Johnson echoed, touching the bow on her own flowered bonnet.

"Thank you." Mary smiled, struggling to focus on Miss Lilly Johnson's long, thin face rather than her overdone bonnet. She hadn't realized that flower-explosion chapeaus were the rage this season. Or perhaps, they were just the local fashion.

"May I present my friend and fellow gardener, Timmy Aubrey?" she said.

"The schoolmaster's son?" Bertha Warner bobbed a glance at Eunice Figg.

The exchange was not lost on Mary.

"Yes, indeed. And grateful I am to have them next door. It's very comforting for a woman whose dear husband is serving our country in the military overseas to have the help of such fine neighbors as Timmy and his father."

"I'm sure," Bertha Warner said after a moment's stilted silence.

"Indeed," the thin Miss Lilly Johnson echoed.

Eunice Figg sniffed twice and cleared her throat. "I assume Sheriff Jane told you of our mission."

"She did say you might be calling," Mary said. "Goodness, where are our manners?" she exclaimed, turning to Timmy. "Won't you ladies come in for tea?"

"We wouldn't want to impose," Eunice Figg said, already halfway up the walk.

"No, indeed," Miss Lilly Johnson echoed, elbowing past Bertha Warner. "I've always wanted to see inside the late Mrs. Armitage's cottage," she confided.

I suppose I'll have to die before it's thought of as Mary Smith's cottage.

Mary hurried up the steps with Timmy at her heels and

ushered the triumvirate through the front door. "You ladies just make yourselves at home."

While she prepared the tea and directed Timmy to wash his hands and lay out cookies on her best china platter, she could hear her guests in the living room.

"Classic arts and crafts decor," Bertha Warner pronounced.

"I love the way the soft rose pattern is carried out in the wallpaper and the fabrics of the curtains and upholstery," Miss Lilly Johnson said.

"William Morris design. Imported!" Eunice Figg's tone rang with authority.

Mary smiled.

"I do believe those curtains are Scottish lace," Bertha Warner observed.

"And the way she's picked up the soft pastels of the room in the bouquet on that lovely carved table in the entry. So artistic," said Miss Lilly Johnson.

Mary decided that of the three she had more of an affinity for Miss Lilly Johnson. At least she seemed more moved by artistry than celebrity.

Some notes from the upright piano floated into the kitchen. "Lovely rosewood. Steinway. No finer name than that," Eunice Figg said.

"And in good tune," Miss Lilly Johnson observed.

"That's a blessing," Bertha Warner commented. "I hate to see a fine instrument not well maintained."

Mary leaned over to Timmy and whispered, "I think we've given them time enough alone. You carry the cookies; I'll handle the tray."

Eunice Figg and Bertha Warner settled side by side on the settee, Miss Lilly Johnson on the Queen Anne chair to the right. Mary and Timmy perched on the matching tufted chairs on the other side of the burl walnut coffee table on which Mary had set the tray.

"It looks like Maison china," Bertha Warner said as Mary

passed her a cup of tea and an embroidered linen napkin.

Without waiting for a reply, holding the pale yellow, floral-painted teacup handle between thumb and index finger, pinky extended, Bertha Warner turned the saucer over to check for herself.

"You have a good eye," Mary said, biting her proverbial tongue.

"Timmy, will you please pass the cookies?" she asked when tea had been served—Timmy's own cup of mostly milk and a teaspoon of sugar.

"Now, ladies, what is your mission?" Mary asked, lifting her cup.

"Well." Eunice Figg sniffed and cleared her throat. "We all voted last meeting to invite you to become a member of the Whispering Bluff Garden Club."

Mary returned her cup to its saucer. "I'm greatly honored."

Bertha Warner put down the cookie she'd been munching. "We were hoping that in accepting our invitation you would be willing to let us have our annual spring tea in your home—"

"Your *lovely* home." Miss Lilly Johnson leaned forward.

"In two weeks," Bertha Warner finished.

"Two weeks. I see." Mary returned her cup to the silver tray. She straightened and folded her hands in her lap.

Three pairs of eyes registered anxious anticipation at her hesitation.

She turned to Timmy. "What do you think, Timmy? Do you think we can handle this honor?"

Timmy returned her smile.

She lifted her gaze. "Timmy and I accept with pleasure."

"Children aren't allowed to be members," Miss Lilly Johnson said, her frail voice apologetic. "Particularly boys."

A look passed between Bertha Warner and Eunice Figg, just short of an eye roll.

"However," Eunice Figg boomed out, fixing Timmy with sober regard, "although gentlemen cannot become *regular* members of the Whispering Bluff *Women's* Garden Club, as president, I am sure there shall be no objection to waiving the rules on the day of our annual spring tea."

Mary gazed at Eunice Figg with grateful eyes and smiled.

eleven

Mary felt quite carefree that bright morning in May. The sun was shining, the birds were singing, and Nancy was happy and being well attended in the capable hands of their dear housekeeper, Mrs. Meade.

Mary was ever grateful for Jane's insistence that Mary hire the fine woman. Dear Jane, so insightful and kind, she always seemed to know what people needed and went to any ends to see it was accomplished.

As she snapped the reins, urging Queenie into a trot, she reviewed her errands. First to the seamstress, Mavis Dodd's, to pick up the new dress she had made for the tea. Then Thompson's General Store. She was almost out of sugar, and she could use some vanilla—oh—and a box of raisins for the oatmeal cookies she would be contributing.

It was fortunate that she hadn't learned to prepare the more exotic foods she'd enjoyed in the past, since this one small general store held only the most basic needs, especially when it came to spices.

She sighed. And then there was the one dark spot in the day: the letter she would drop off at the post office, addressed to Col. Clayton Smith. Her deception.

Finally lunch with Jane! That always brightened her spirits.

❧

Mavis clapped her hands as Mary stepped out of the draped alcove that served as a dressing room in Mavis's tiny shop. Her sweet, round face reflected her prideful delight. "Oh, Mary, I don't think I have to alter a single spot. It fits you absolutely perfectly."

Mary posed for a moment like one of those models sketched

in the Butterick pattern book; then she twirled with a giggle, the formfitting flared skirt, with its slight bustle, swinging gracefully around her ankles.

"The cut is just right for you," Mavis said. "I knew it would be, with that little nipped-in waist, and those lovely, voluptuous leg-o'-mutton sleeves, and that touch of lace at the throat and the cuffs." Mavis continued to enthuse, admiring her handiwork. "Jonquil yellow is definitely your color! It's just scrumptious with your violet eyes." She stepped forward and straightened the hem then stepped back, clasping her hands to her breast. "You look like a china doll—a veritable china doll!"

"With dirty fingernails." Mary laughed, spreading her hands. "I spend so much time in the flower beds lately I doubt I'll ever get them clean again."

"Is the skirt comfortable? Not too tight at the waist? Don't tell me if it is. I don't want to know. You look so lovely I'd hate to have to change a stitch."

"Don't worry, Mavis, the dress is perfect! I love it. Now what do I owe you for this masterpiece?" Mary asked as she disappeared to change behind the drape.

When she emerged, Mavis handed her a bill for seven dollars and twenty-five cents. "That includes the lining and the lace."

Mary looked at it, her mouth dropping in mock surprise. "This is outrageous!" Then she giggled. "In Chicago it would be three times as much and half as pretty."

"You came from Chicago? I didn't know that."

Mary's heart lurched. "A hundred years ago," she said lightly, handing Mavis some bills and quickly changing the subject. "Thank you, thank you, my dear. I know you did double duty to get this done in time and ready for the tea. And I promise to extol your praises for every compliment I anticipate. I'll be your walking advertisement." Mary plopped her straw bowler atop her dark chignon.

"You don't have to do that, Mary." Mavis smiled. "It's not like there's any competition. I'm the only seamstress in Whispering Bluff."

"Nevertheless." Mary slipped on her gloves.

"Everybody's talking about the event, you know," Mavis said as she began to wrap the dress carefully in folds of tissue. "I wouldn't be surprised if there were thirty ladies. They're not only anxious to admire your garden but—"

"I know, see inside Mrs. Armitage's house. Lilly Johnson let that cat out of the bag."

"Well, that, too," Mavis said, tying the box with a satin ribbon and handing it to Mary. "Oh, by the way, you don't know somebody who might want a puppy? My Hildy dropped a litter a few weeks ago. Of course they won't be weaned for a while, but I'm looking to find them homes eventually."

"Nancy's a little young to appreciate a puppy," Mary said, "but I have a neighbor—"

"The schoolmaster."

Mary nodded. "His little boy would probably love one. I can't tell about the father, though." She shrugged. "But you never know."

A half hour later, as she was tucking her purchases from Thompson's under the seat of the phaeton, Mary heard a familiar voice.

"Yoo-hoo, Mary!" Jane was waving from in front of her office at the jail. She looked both ways, lifted her skirt, and hurried across the street.

"What have you there?" Mary asked, glancing down at the rolled sheaf of papers tucked under Jane's arm.

"WANTED posters. The courier just delivered them."

"I hope my face isn't among them," Mary said lightly, shivering at the very real possibility.

"Only if you have a beard. It seems the River Gang robbed a bank in Weld County." Jane stepped up onto the boardwalk. "I doubt they'd bother with Whispering Bluff. But I suppose you never know. They robbed three banks between Pueblo and Denver, and it looks like they're heading our way. She pushed open the post office door. "We don't need that kind of excitement," she said. "Morning, Henrietta."

The postmistress glanced up from her sorting and glared with her beady eyes at the claw hammer Jane was holding. "What's that you've got there?"

"WANTED posters. The River Gang."

"See that you don't make big holes in the plaster," the older woman said, pointing a long, bony finger, "like you did last time. We just had the wall patched and painted."

"And a fetching color, too," Jane said, wrinkling her nose at the faded khaki wash. She began unrolling the posters on the high counter.

"Good morning, Miss Henrietta," Mary said in her most bland voice as she pushed the lying envelope across the counter.

"I suppose it's another one of your love letters to the Philippines."

Mary nodded, determined not to let another lying word pass her lips.

"How many does that make?" Henrietta frowned.

Mary could see her ticking the number off in her brain.

"Three. That's right, three," Henrietta pronounced.

Jane winked at Mary. "You're sure it's not just two? Or maybe four?" She picked up a poster.

"Three!" the postmistress said, her lips pursed with irritation that her veracity might be questioned. "And not a single letter in return. One would think—"

Jane began loudly hammering up the poster.

"I'm sure he has more pressing things on his mind," Mary said mildly. "He's never been much of a letter writer. But I feel I must send mine, anyway."

"Still," Henrietta sniffed, "you'd think he'd somehow find the time to write his wife, if he really loved her."

How disheartening that would be if it were true. Mary lowered her gaze. But then it was. Her husband could not have loved her less. She had the scars to prove it. Absently she touched her cheek.

Jane gave the nail a final and deliberate bang.

"Watch it," Henrietta growled, glancing up from examining Mary's envelope.

Jane came back to the counter and grabbed the second poster. Then suddenly she paused. "Really, Henrietta, why would you say something so hurtful to Mary?"

"Like what?"

"You know like what."

Mary interrupted. "Please, Jane, it doesn't matter. I'm sure she didn't mean anything by it."

"It does matter." Jane turned back to the postmistress whose gray hair was pulled back into that painfully tight bun—a reason, perhaps, for her perpetually ill humor. "When you say things like, 'He would write if he really loved her,' that hurts people's feelings and makes them sad. Besides, everybody knows that the mail gets all mixed up in wartime. Why, he could have written dozens of letters that never got here. I just pray he's received Mary's."

"I only speak the truth," Henrietta retorted. "If it hurts, I'm sorry." She sounded more offended than contrite, but she did turn to Mary and mumble, "I beg your forgiveness if I hurt your feelings."

"It's all right, Miss Henrietta. No offense taken."

Jane sighed audibly, grabbed the final poster, and returned to the wall.

Mary followed, absently watching her.

Jane may be pounding nails, but the postmistress had hit one nail squarely on the head. No love had ever been lost between Mary and her erstwhile husband. Maybe the shrewd woman had sensed that, although Mary couldn't imagine how.

"All in a day's work," Jane said, standing back and observing the gallery of bearded felons. "They look mean, don't they? Especially that one in the middle."

Mary shuddered at the finely drawn sketch. She'd seen cold eyes like that before. Too often! She was reminded, again, that she could never have exposed her precious Nancy to Clayton's unpredictable and vicious violence. And though she was, in all likelihood, a hunted person like those on the posters, her child was well worth the sacrifice she'd made.

After one last look at her handiwork, Jane turned to Mary. "My tummy tells me it's time for lunch." At the door, she paused. "Sorry for losing my temper, Henrietta," she said, sounding no more contrite than the postmistress had.

Beneath the spreading chestnut in the corner of Jane's garden, Mary leaned her head against the back of the wicker garden chair, drowsy from the afternoon sun and sumptuous repast of delicate tea sandwiches, mixed fruit cup, scones slathered with crème fraîche, and Jane's famous homemade lemon curd.

The sweet girl was quite perfect in every way. It never ceased to surprise Mary that some man hadn't snatched her up.

"All I can make is a reasonably decent oatmeal cookie." Sighing, Mary broke off a bit of scone and popped it into her mouth. "I don't suppose you'd share the recipe for this lemon curd?"

"Of course I will. I always share my recipes. Then if I lose one I know where to find it."

Mary smiled at her friend. "I love being here, Jane. It's so beautiful and peaceful. You've really created an intimate paradise: the flowers, the blooming lilac, the roses." She took a deep breath. "And it smells soooo good."

"God's perfume."

Yes, the woman was absolutely perfect. "And to think this little bit of sun-dappled heaven lies right next door to a jail."

"The sacred and the profane."

"I'm surprised the garden club didn't have their tea here in your paradise."

"My wee paradise? Even if it were large enough, it's not affixed to Mrs. Armitage's Queen Anne cottage."

"No more lovely a cottage exists than yours. It's perfection inside and out. You have a God-given instinct for the womanly arts. There's no doubt about it."

"Then why. . ." Jane's soulful gaze drifted to her glass of lemonade. "Look at you. You're younger than I am—"

"By eight months."

"And you have a husband and a baby. And here I am a spinster."

"*Oh, please.* At twenty-three?"

"With few prospects."

"You have lots of beaux."

"But none I'd want to take home to Daddy, God rest his soul." She shook her head sadly.

"Don't be in a hurry, darling. You have to live with your choice for a very long time."

"I'm afraid there aren't a whole lot of prospects in Whispering Bluff. . .Except maybe. . .There's always. . ."

Mary knew what was coming.

Jane leaned forward. "What do you really think of John Aubrey?"

"It's hard to know how to answer that. I don't really know him, except as Timmy's father."

"Not as a friend? You live next door to each other."

"He's a very private person."

"Is he a good father?"

"The best I can say is that he tries."

Jane didn't seem to be listening. "He seems so intelligent. Certainly he's handsome."

"He is that."

"In a brooding, mysterious way, the way. . .like. . ."

"Mr. Rochester in *Jane Eyre?*"

"Yes! Exactly! Exactly like Mr. Rochester."

Mary smiled and shook her head. "Oh, Janie, my dear. You are such a romantic. Now think about it. Would you really want Mr. Rochester to be the father of your children?"

Mary was amused by her conversation with Jane, but it made her sad, too. Sad that Jane could harbor such fantasies about so flawed a hero. And sad for John Aubrey's sake that he couldn't be the hero who Jane needed.

twelve

Mary was nothing if not organized. Her endless lists had been checked off. Along with Mrs. Meade, she had cleaned and polished, she had laid out the linens and the silver tea service and the fine china. She and Hitch—and Timmy—had manicured the bowers of flowers until there was not a dead blossom or brown leaf to be seen. Now, all that was left were those things that could only be done at the very last minute.

The stage was set. The play was about to begin.

Standing on her back porch that dew-kissed Saturday morning, just two days before the tea, Mary breathed in the cool, scented air, basking in the sun's early rays. Her heart was filled with gratitude for all with which the Lord had blessed her: her baby, her home, her beautiful garden, and the opportunity to share it with her new friends.

She slid her hand over the rail, still damp with dew, and ambled down the back steps, glancing over at the house across the way. Soon Timmy would be running across the yard.

She smiled and turned.

Suddenly her breath clogged in her throat.

"My garden!" she howled.

Along the side of the cottage, she saw only dirt and rubble and stubs down to the nub. Standing in the middle of it all, tether dangling from its neck, the schoolmaster's goat, chewing, contented as you please.

Like a madwoman, she raced toward the brazen beast. She grabbed the creature's rope and began dragging it across the yard, through the copse of mulberry trees until, breathless, she reached the schoolmaster's back stoop.

"John Aubrey," she railed, "you get out here!"

She tied the rope to a porch post and rushed up the steps. She pounded on the back door with both fists, shrieking, "John Aubrey, I'll never forgive you for this! Come out here now, John Aubrey, you coward. Come out—"

The door opened suddenly, and her fist found his chest. "Oh. . .oh. . ." She couldn't catch her breath. She couldn't speak. She could only sob and gasp.

"What—"

She slapped away his appeasing hand. "D–d–don't–t. . .touch me," she cried. "You are the most—the most irresponsible man in the world. Y–your goat. . ." She pointed a trembling finger toward her cottage. "Y–your goat ate my garden."

Fueled by fury and frustration, she glared up at him. "Can't you take care of anything? First it's your boy; now it's your goat. You're—you're. . .You're impossible!"

She was just beginning to get started, when suddenly she caught sight of Timmy cowering behind his father's legs.

Oh no! Timmy!

She bent down, stricken. "Oh, my dear, don't be upset; I'm not angry with you. It's not your fault." She touched his shoulder. "Don't worry, darling, please. Everything will be all right. Maybe we'll just. . .we'll just stake that old goat out there in the flower bed with a sign around her neck, FLOWERS INSIDE."

What I'd really like to do is stake his father out there.

"Now, don't you worry, dear."

Running out of words and the ability to further control her ire and her tongue, she rose abruptly and, throwing John Aubrey a scathing look, swung around and stomped down the steps, through the trees, and across her yard.

What would the garden club ladies think of her lovely landscape now?

❧

In shock John stood in the doorway gazing after her.

Behind him he heard Timmy's anguished sobbing, and looked down.

He wanted to say, *See what happens when you disobey and let the goat out of the yard?* But he couldn't; the boy was too distraught.

John squatted down and drew his son into his arms. He could feel the small body quiver against him and hot tears soak his shirt. His first tears since his mother had died.

Suddenly he was aware of how natural it seemed, embracing his boy that way. How long had it been since he'd felt the clinging warmth of his child in his arms? Or even wanted to feel it?

He could hardly remember.

"There, there, Timmy. Don't cry. We'll think of something."

Timmy sniffed and pulled back, a hopeful expression rising in his liquid brown eyes.

John stood up, resting his hand on the boy's shoulder. "The first thing is to get Myrtle locked in her yard. Since you let her out, I think you're a big enough boy to take her back."

Timmy nodded and bounded down the steps. He untied the goat and, with John bringing up the rear, pulled her into the enclosed yard beside the horse stall.

"Don't forget to lock the gate," John reminded him.

But Timmy had already reached up and engaged the latch.

As they walked back to the house, John could see the havoc across the way. It looked like a cyclone had struck a long narrow path. He glanced down at his son. All caused by the disobedience of one small boy. He sighed. And, he supposed, the carelessness of one father, for not keeping a better eye on him.

He didn't blame Mary Smith for being angry.

Although angry hardly described it!

He wondered what Joanna would have done. How would she have handled a situation like this?

Not with the same vitriol as Mary Smith, that was for sure.

But then Joanna wouldn't have been having the tea in the first place. She was timid, rarely extended herself to those outside her family. She had always depended on John for her interests and entertainment.

He felt a gentle tug on his shirt and looked down into Timmy's expectant eyes.

"Give me time, son. I'll come up with something." His gaze fell again on the devastation.

And the tea party was Monday afternoon.

He sat down on his back steps and rested his elbows on his knees.

For several minutes, he and Timmy sat side by side in silence. Finally John mused, half to himself and half to his son, "You know, Timmy, I think I know someone who might be able to help us."

❧

"Come on in, gentlemen," Jane called cheerily through her kitchen window.

Jane's house was next door to the jail, on the corner of Main and First, across from the bank.

"You and Timmy are just in time to sample the cookies I'm making for the garden club tea."

John and Timmy pushed through the arbored side gate and entered what everyone in town referred to as "Jane's little paradise."

Yes, we've come to the right place, John thought, eyeing the abundance of foxgloves and petunias. He even noticed other plants that he didn't know the names of that had also graced Mary Smith's garden.

Jane would surely know what to do.

She met them at the back door, ushering them through the porch into her kitchen, redolent with the aroma of cinnamon and nutmeg and the tangy, tart scent of lemon.

The walls were painted a soft canary yellow, reflecting the sunny disposition of the sweet sheriff, herself. Although John had trouble thinking of her as such, she was so feminine and dainty. Even her ruffled apron covered in flour dust added to her appealing domesticity.

On the trestle table in the middle of the room sat trays mounded with a variety of tarts and cookies, and as she spoke, Jane stacked a platter with a fresh batch from the oven.

"Sit down," she enjoined. "Maybe you'd prefer a scone with some of my famous lemon curd instead of one of my even more famous ginger cookies." She giggled. "What do you think, Timmy?"

He pointed at the ginger cookies.

"I suspected as much." She smiled beguilingly at John. "And you, kind sir?"

As he had before, he recognized an invitation in her warm regard that he could never bring himself to acknowledge. He was neither a man worthy of such goodness nor welcoming of such fond attention, and she was entirely too innocent and ingenuous a lady to encourage.

Still, he wanted to please her. "One of each, thank you, Miss Jane. With an extra dollop of that lemon curd."

She turned and pulled two china plates and two glasses from the cupboard.

The woman was even willing to trust china to four-year-old hands.

"What are ginger cookies without cold milk?" Jane pronounced, disappearing into the back porch and returning in short order with a frothing pitcher from the icebox.

When both Timmy and John had been served, she sat down across the table, gazing at them, her eyes rapt with pleasure as she watched them. She offered seconds and thirds, which Timmy eagerly accepted and John didn't have the heart to refuse, though he sensed he was leading her on.

"Mary tells me you've been a fine help in her garden," she said to Timmy.

Timmy glanced at John.

John swallowed, wiped his mouth with his napkin, and cleared his throat. "Actually, that's why we're here."

Jane looked at Timmy in mock surprise and blinked flirtatiously at John. "You mean you didn't come because of my ginger cookies?"

"Those, too." John smiled and took a deep breath. "But I'm afraid there's been a catastrophe."

"A catastrophe?"

Timmy nodded.

John continued. "Myrtle, Timmy's goat, escaped and destroyed the garden on the north side of Mary Smith's cottage."

"Oh no!" Jane's eyes widened. "That *is* a catastrophe."

Timmy nodded, guilt stamped across his young face.

John rested a hand on Timmy's shoulder. "We—Timmy and I—thought you might have an idea. . . ."

"Indeed I do." Jane snapped to her feet. "We'll just have to dig up flowers from my garden and plant them in hers. There's little time. We must hurry."

"But. . ." John intended no serious protest, since that had been his thought from the beginning, but at least he felt obliged to offer one.

"No buts about it," Jane said. "Mary is having the garden club tea; I am not. We must get those plants transferred before dark."

"Under the circumstances, we gratefully accept. But we certainly don't expect you to help."

"Nonsense." Jane whipped off her apron. "There are spades and boxes in the shed. I'll be out when I've changed into something more appropriate," she called over her shoulder as she disappeared down the hall.

But just as John was loading the final box of snapdragons into the buckboard, Deputy Spike Terrell lumbered over in a real hurry from the office. "Just got a teletype, Sheriff. The River Gang's struck again. In Eagle this time."

Jane frowned. "They're getting closer."

"Seems the sheriff there's forming a posse and wants us to bring some men."

"Oh dear." Jane looked sincerely disappointed. "I hate to

leave you, when I promised to help." Then she shrugged. "But duty calls."

John could see the light of excitement shining in her eyes.

"It's my first posse as sheriff," she confided.

He smiled as he watched her hurry into the house. What a generous, adorable, spunky little soul she was—and such a sweet disposition, too.

Quite the opposite from his neighbor, Mary Smith.

thirteen

Nothing Mary accomplished all morning seemed to matter in light of the disaster. And here she was again, pacing the kitchen, struggling to control her rage.

That man, that John Aubrey, had ruined everything with his carelessness and his indifference.

All those ladies visiting her cottage the day after tomorrow, expecting perfection—and what would they get? An entire strip of barren ground, a bleak wasteland!

Viewing it once more out her kitchen window, she couldn't hold back the tears. She had staked so much on this party, invested so much. She'd given it her very best.

She had every right to be angry. Who wouldn't be?

She hiccuped and wiped her eyes.

So why do I also feel so guilty?

She plopped down and folded her hands on the table.

Timmy was the reason.

It was catching sight of Timmy that had brought her up short, that poor little boy, crying and quaking behind his father.

In fairness, she hadn't known Timmy was there.

Where else would she expect him to be?

She buried her head in her hands.

Not to mention that she had demeaned John Aubrey in front of his son with her ranting censure. Regardless of what she thought of the man or how much he deserved it, attacking him in front of his boy was wrong. And it was not the first time, she thought, with guilty remembrance. She'd done as much when she had found Timmy running toward the woods two months ago.

Had it only been that long?

As she sat there, considering the damage her temper had done, weighed against the damage done to her garden, things took on a different perspective.

If the truth be told, what really interested the garden club ladies was seeing the inside of old Mrs. Armitage's cottage. Her garden was just the excuse. If she deftly guided where they walked, they probably wouldn't even notice the missing flowers on the side of the house.

What was important was that she had said some really hurtful things to John Aubrey, which he probably would never forgive and which could seriously jeopardize her relationship with Timmy.

She couldn't let that happen. The child had become too precious to her. For Timmy's sake, if for no other, she had to apologize to John Aubrey.

Which did seem a bit ironic, given that the man's goat had started it all.

By the time she had mustered up her courage, it was near noon. With Nancy in her arms, she trudged across the lot to her neighbor's house and knocked on the back door, politely.

No answer.

Again.

Still no answer.

Well, who could blame him?

Discouraged, she turned to leave then realized that his horse was missing from the corral. And so was the buckboard.

Somewhat relieved that the nonresponse to her knock could not be construed as a personal rebuff, she plodded home through the trees.

By the time lunch was behind her, she felt so emotionally drained, rehearsing her inevitable encounter with John Aubrey, that she could hardly wait for Nancy's afternoon nap, more for her own sake than the baby's.

Wearily she dropped onto her bed next to Nancy's crib and fell at once to sleep.

Almost immediately, it seemed, she was awakened by voices on the far side of the house. Who could that possibly be?

Quietly, so as not to wake Nancy, she crept out of the bedroom, down the stairs, and hurried out into the backyard.

She saw the buckboard first, filled with blooms. Then, beneath the kitchen window, John Aubrey and Timmy, kneeling side by side in the dirt, filling the decimated plot with flowering plants.

All she could do was burst into tears.

John Aubrey turned and, seeing her, leaped to his feet and rushed over. "It wasn't our intention to make you cry."

"How can I help it?" she sobbed. "Look at this wonderful, incredible thing you and Timmy have done." And she broke into another paroxysm of tears.

"Thanks to your friend, Sheriff Jane McKee. She wanted to be here to help, too, but she had pressing sheriff business."

"Oh, dear Janie," Mary wept. "That doesn't surprise me at all about her. But you, after the way I behaved. . ."

She felt his comforting hand on her arm. This time she did not slap it away. Instead, she looked up into his kind, smiling eyes. "Oh, John Aubrey, I am so sorry for all the cruel things I said to you."

He gave her a chagrined smile. "With some elements of truth."

"Only small ones." She took his dirt-caked hand in both of hers. "I just want you to know that I was going to apologize, anyway, even before. . ." She scanned the transformation already taking place. "Even before all this. In fact, I went over to your house earlier, but no one answered. And I didn't blame you. And then I saw the buckboard was gone and. . ." She took a deep sighing breath. "I had no right to talk to you the way I did, especially in front of Timmy. I just feel so terrible. I shouldn't have lost my temper that way."

John Aubrey lifted a brow. "Are you applying for sainthood, too?"

She cocked her head. *Oh yes. He'd just come from Jane's.*

"Under the circumstances, only a saint could have taken the high road, Mary Smith, and *that* I will never accuse you of being. As fine a woman as you are, alas, you are quite human. . . . And thankfully so!"

Mary sniffed. "You're being charitable."

"I'm being honest." He smiled, that wonderful smile of his with the flashing teeth and the crinkles around his soulful brown eyes.

"Can you forgive me?" she begged.

"What is it Jesus said? 'Judge not, and ye shall not be judged: condemn not, and ye shall not be condemned: forgive, and ye shall be forgiven.' I think it is in my best interest to do so."

Mary dropped his hand. "Why, John Aubrey, I didn't know you were a churchgoer."

He gave her an odd look and shrugged. "I guess my past is catching up with me." Abruptly he turned. "Well, I'd better get back to work if we're going to get this finished by sundown."

"I'll just be a minute." Mary ran back into the house, scooped up Nancy from her crib, and returned to the yard. She spread a quilt under the oak and laid Nancy on it with her favorite stuffed bunny and a cracker to nibble on. Then she went over and knelt down next to Timmy. With reliable old Hitch joining them, too, the garden returned to its former splendor long before the sun had set.

"You must let me make your supper," Mary said, dusting her hands together. "It's the least I can do."

"That's usually my line." John Aubrey smiled.

She wished he'd stop being so nice. It was getting quite disconcerting.

"You're invited, too, Hitch," she said, picking up Nancy. She handed her to John Aubrey and proceeded to fold the quilt.

Hitch yanked on his ear. "Thank ya, Miss Mary, but I have plans for the evenin'—it being Saturday night, and all."

"Why, Hitch, you're blushing. All right, then, you're excused."

She couldn't resist adding an aside to John. "He gets better fare at Trudy St. Cyr's boardinghouse."

The bowlegged man grinned and sauntered away with the self-conscious gait of one who knew he was being talked about.

As she and John returned to the house, Mary said, "I hope you don't expect too much of my supper, John Aubrey. I'm not the fine cook Janie is. That woman makes an art out of homemaking, every aspect of it. Look at these flowers. You can see how lucky I am to have her as a best friend. We all are. She's so generous and sweet." Mary sighed and hung her head in mock despair. "Not moody and mean like me."

With Nancy in his arms and Timmy at his heels, John Aubrey clomped up the stairs behind Mary. "Only once in a while," he murmured.

"I heard that," Mary laughed, pushing open the back door and reaching for her baby.

᛫᛫

By the time Timmy and John returned from washing up and changing into clean clothes, Mary had done the same, looking fresh and lovely in a green-striped dress that complemented her extraordinary eyes.

"Wave night-night to the gentlemen, Nancy," Mary said, standing in the door to the hallway with her darling infant.

John couldn't help smiling as the baby gurgled and dimpled, delighted that her mama had taken her hand and waved it.

When the two had disappeared up the stairs, John turned to Timmy. "I remember when you were that age, Timmy. That's one cute baby." He leaned closer and whispered, "But you were just as cute. And smart! You were saying words by the time you were eight months old." He put his arm around the boy. "You were probably the smartest baby I ever saw. I'm not saying that just because I'm your dad. Everybody thought so."

A small, prideful smile played about Timmy's lips.

"God made you special, Timmy. Never forget it."

Now where did that come from? God in the picture, and twice in one day.

Mary bustled back into the kitchen. "Well, she's down, but not yet out," she said lightly, smiling at him. "I expect she will be soon. It's been a long day. . .for both of us."

When she smiled that way, her head tilted, her violet eyes twinkling, her lovely mouth just slightly open as if laughter might bubble out at a moment's notice to surprise him, he felt himself respond in quite an unexpected way.

Even against his will. Certainly against his better judgment! Quickly he got his thoughts in check.

While Mary had been upstairs, John had stoked the fire in the stove.

"That was very thoughtful of you, John," she said, putting a pot with chicken and noodles on the plate to simmer. "Janie would have added all sorts of interesting herbs and spices. She just has an instinct for those things." Mary shrugged. "I'm just a simple cook."

"Simple is fine," John assured her.

He watched as she whipped up some biscuits and put them in the oven and snapped the ends off the green beans. He offered to slice the tomatoes. "We bachelors are very handy. You'd be surprised."

But she demurred and countered, "You and Timmy can set the table. He knows where everything is. Don't you, Timmy?"

She may not be a fancy cook, John thought, *but she's very efficient in the kitchen. No wasted motions.* And actually the plates she served looked quite tempting with the chicken, the green beans, the tomatoes—

"And the sprig of parsley for color, like my aunt Hannah taught me," she said.

When they were seated, Mary reached across the table. "John, will you say the blessing?"

He hesitated. He didn't want to be rude, but it had been a long time. He wasn't quite sure what was expected.

He glanced over at Timmy who was already grasping Mary's hand and was now reaching for his father's.

John closed his large hand around the boy's small paw.

Then a strange thing happened.

It was as if an electric charge from that little hand shot straight into John's heart.

He gazed down into Timmy's expectant eyes. *Now what?*

He bowed his head.

And then the short, familiar prayer came as if he'd said it yesterday. "Dear Lord, bless this food to our use and us to Thy service. And make us ever mindful of the needs of others. And, Lord, thank You for giving Timmy and me the opportunity to be good neighbors. Amen."

Timmy pulled his hand away at once, but Mary's lingered. As she withdrew, she smiled at John. "Short and sweet! Dinner will definitely not get cold." She pulled her napkin into her lap. "Well, neighbor, I think it's time we put aside all this Mary Smith and John Aubrey business and got down to just plain Mary and John. What do you think, Timmy?"

Timmy grinned his approval and nodded.

"That's *Miss* Mary to you, young man," his father said with mock sternness.

Mary. Nice name. A no-nonsense name, like the lady herself. And it has a smile in it when you say the word. Not like John, where your mouth goes long and serious.

"What are you thinking?" Mary gave him an oblique look as she picked up her fork.

"What am I thinking? Well, I'm thinking, Mary, Mary, quite contrary, how does your garden grow?"

Laughing, she joined in. "With silver bells and cockle shells and pretty maids all in a row."

It would be hard to find a maid prettier than you, Mary Smith, with dark ringlets wisping around your brow and laughing amethyst eyes that light up a room and a smile designed to melt a man's heart.

One would have to search aplenty to find a maid to match you.

But he dared not say it aloud.

fourteen

"Part of me is looking forward to the garden party and part of me will be awfully glad when it's over," Mary said, pouring hot water into the teapot and carrying it to the table.

"As far as I can see, everything looks just about perfect," John assured her, placing the last dish on the pile that he had finished drying. "Especially your side garden."

She cocked her head and sent him a sidewise glance as she slid into her chair opposite Timmy at the table. "I'm counting on your help, Timmy."

Timmy made a face.

"I know you're shy, but remember, Mrs. Figg made you a special invitation. Besides, I need you to be my courage, like you were when the ladies first came to visit."

Timmy slouched down and nodded reluctantly.

John dropped into the chair next to him. "You can wear your new shoes, son." He gave Mary a teasing smile. "That should give Miss Mary comfort."

"All Timmy needs is his winning smile," she replied archly. "But shiny new shoes would be nice."

She poured herself and John a cup of tea and two table-spoons full for Timmy in a cup that she filled with warm milk, adding a teaspoon of sugar.

"Shall we tell Miss Mary what special day is coming up, Timmy?" John asked.

Timmy nodded.

"Timmy's birthday."

Mary clapped her hands and focused her attention on the child. "When?"

"The twenty-ninth," John said.

"Will school be out? Is that a Saturday? Oh Timmy, I'm so excited. Do I get to give the birthday party?"

She looked at John, who looked at Timmy, who nodded with such vigor he almost fell off the chair.

"Have you thought of who you're going to invite?" Mary asked.

Timmy glanced at his father.

"Mrs. Grice, our housekeeper," John said.

"And surely Sheriff Janie," Mary added. "I'll bet she'd make the birthday cake if we asked. Believe me, she makes a better birthday cake than I could even imagine in my dreams. Of course that wouldn't be the only reason to ask her. . . . Even though it probably would be chocolate. . .with chocolate frosting."

Timmy grinned.

"Very good. Then she's on the list. I know she'll be thrilled."

That was an understatement. Jane wouldn't miss the opportunity to demonstrate her culinary skills for John. . .and Timmy, of course.

"I think Mrs. Meade would like to come, as well. She loves Timmy. Who else, John?"

"Nancy."

"Of course, Nancy and me. Nancy never goes anyplace without me. Besides, I'm giving the party. . . . Have I left anyone out?"

Timmy bounced on his chair and pointed at his father.

"Are you sure you want to invite him?" Mary frowned.

Giggling, Timmy nodded fiercely.

"I still think someone is missing," John said.

Timmy hopped out of his chair and jumped up and down, pointing at himself.

"I don't know, John; he's awfully young."

"He'll be five soon."

Mary slapped her forehead and looked heavenward. "Oh, I forgot. Of course. Five-year-olds should certainly attend birthday parties." She wrinkled her nose at Timmy. "Especially if it's their own."

Pushing the platter of cookies toward him, she murmured, "Janie would probably have had a cream pie on hand instead of these plain old oatmeal cookies."

John crossed his arms and fixed her with a level gaze. "Mary, I'm perplexed. I've noticed that you never miss an opportunity to endorse Miss Jane. Is there a reason here, one that I'm missing?"

"What do you mean?" Mary asked innocently, lifting her cup of tea.

"I think we both know what I mean."

Mary sighed. "All right, John." She reached for a cookie. "I admit, there was a time when I wouldn't even have considered you as a person worthy of my sweet friend. But now I realize you're quite a different man than I first surmised." She looked at him directly. "Now I see that you have—how can I put this? I can see that you have very definite potential."

Humor drew up the corners of his mouth.

"It's not funny, John. I'm quite serious."

"I can see you are." The mirth had reached his eyes. He leaned forward. "Just so you understand, I'm not ready to have someone special in my life just now."

"You may not, but there are those who count on you." She shot a quick glance at Timmy.

"He has you," John said quietly, suddenly serious.

"But—"

"No more, Mary!" He wasn't smiling now. "I'm not ready. And to be honest, I see little possibility of changing my mind anytime in the near future. If ever."

She studied the tea leaves floating in the bottom of her cup. "You think I've overstepped."

He didn't answer.

"You're angry with me."

"No. I think you have the best intentions. But I'm not ready,

Mary. When I am, I'll let you know."

Mary felt flustered and self-conscious. She didn't know what to say. Nervously she plucked a crumb from the table.

Relieving her of the necessity of speaking, John asked, "May I have another one of those delicious, nutritious oatmeal cookies?"

"By all means."

After several minutes of silence, Mary sighed. "I do have one talent you might not know about. Other than baking fine oatmeal cookies, that is."

"And gardening and—"

"That's enough, John." She made a face at him and hopped up from the table. "Follow me, gentlemen."

&

If he were to be interested in a woman, Jane McKee would *not* be the one he would choose, John thought, watching the sway of Mary's lithe figure as he followed her up the hall into her parlor.

She sat down in front of the carved, upright piano and pushed up the panel that covered the keyboard. Smiling at Timmy, she allowed her fingers to dance lightly over the keys, picking out random chords. "You didn't know I could play the piano, did you?"

He shook his head.

"I must start making it a habit to bring music into my home again, for Nancy's sake." She glanced up at John. "It meant so much to me as a child."

John pulled over a chair from the game table beneath the front window and sat down where he could observe them both, his son and the woman.

The woman. Mary Smith. . .Mary.

Oh yes, there was no doubt whom he would choose, despite her passionate nature.

Or maybe because of it.

She engaged his imagination. She made him feel alive again.

If he had a choice. . .

But he didn't.

His gaze fell on the gold band on the ring finger of Mary's left hand, winking in the light from the lamp atop the piano.

The gold band, her tether to the man of whom he'd rarely heard her speak. Not that she would to him nor that he would want her to.

The gold band that had been one of the reasons John had originally thought her perfect for his purpose. Insulating him from expectations and demands that he was incapable, or unwilling, to make, either to his son. . .or a woman.

Nothing about her had changed.

Only he had changed.

"It's been a long time since I've had an audience," Mary said, absently picking out a familiar harmony. "I'll bet you know this one, Timmy." Softly she began to sing as her fingers found the notes: " 'Jesus, tender Shepherd, hear me; bless thy little lamb tonight; through the darkness be Thou near me; Keep me safe till morning light.' "

She smiled at him. "Do you remember that one, Timmy?"

He nodded and drew close, resting his head on her shoulder as his eyes followed the movement of her hands.

" 'All this day Thy hand has led me, and I thank Thee for Thy care. . . .' "

John was captivated by her clear contralto, her true pitch, her expressive tone. It was a voice one could never tire of hearing.

" 'Thou hast clothed me, warmed and fed me, listen to my evening prayer.' "

She looked up at him. "I suspect you know the words, John; join me."

"I'm not much of a singer."

She continued, her gaze holding his. " 'Let my sins be all forgiven; bless the friends I love so well. . . .' " Then she smiled and cast her eyes down. " 'Take me when I die to heaven, happy there with Thee to dwell.' "

Her hands rested on the keys as the final notes echoed in the silence. Then she met his gaze again, her expression filled with the utmost warmth and regard.

What was this woman doing to him?

Abruptly he said, "Timmy is—Timmy was the singer in our family. Weren't you, Timmy?"

His son turned away, burying his face in Mary's shoulder.

Mary caressed his cheek. "One day you'll sing again."

Ah yes, John had wanted things perfect for his son, and perfect he'd gotten. Only he wasn't included in the picture.

Stunned at the direction his thoughts had taken, he turned away. He was tired, that was all. It had been a long day. *Fatigue plays funny tricks with a man's mind.*

"All right, Timmy," Mary said. "I'm going to try to play something that you don't have to sing. I hope I can still remember it."

With that she began a short sonata by Mozart. When she had finished, she gazed down at him. "Well, what did you think?"

He nodded drowsily and yawned.

"Oh dear, I'm beginning to put my audience to sleep." Giving Timmy a hug, she rose abruptly and covered the keys. Then, with her gorgeous eyes bright, her chin raised, and her head at a determined tilt, she lifted her hand as if to ward off the anticipated adulation. "It's no use, John. No matter how you beg and plead, I will not play an encore."

He wanted to drink in her dark beauty, drown in her violet eyes, breathe in her scented perfume, hear her voice that flowed with the texture and color of thick honey.

He picked up his drowsy son, and averting his eyes for fear they might betray him, he cleared his throat. "Thank you, Mary. This has been a most—a most pleasant evening. I look forward to your favoring us with another concert soon."

"Thank *you*, John; you give me an incentive to practice again."

At the door, she smiled up into his eyes. "I can honestly say, this is a day, I shall *never, ever* forget!"

"Nor I," he said with a huskiness he could not control.

Nor I!

fifteen

That night, weary as she was, Mary had trouble falling asleep. She lay staring into the dark, playing the day back in her mind, from the beginning to the end: the frustration, the forgiveness, and finally—yes, finally—the friendship. For she felt a kinship with John Aubrey that she'd never experienced with any man.

Certainly not with her husband—even in the best of times.

Sitting across from John at the kitchen table had seemed so natural, Timmy there, Nancy safely asleep upstairs. Their conversation over dinner, their teasing banter as he dried the dishes and she made tea.

But her thoughts persisted on how he had responded when she implied that Timmy needed a mother. The look in his eyes when he'd answered, "He has you."

It had disquieted her then. It disquieted her now.

It made her realize that she was, indeed, in danger of feeling too much like the child's mother. She also knew she mustn't allow herself to do so.

Despite his protestations, she had no doubt that once his mourning was past, John, the compassionate, intelligent, amusing John who had emerged, would someday find a wife. And when he did, Timmy would be that woman's son—which was as it should be.

When that day came, she hoped John would see Jane for the treasure that she was. There would be no finer woman for Timmy to call Mother than dear, sweet Jane. It would make the change so much easier for them all if it were she.

Still, Mary couldn't help feeling a twinge of regret knowing that she must not let herself—or Timmy, for that matter—

get so emotionally connected that when that day came the separation would be unduly difficult. Children could get so attached. To say nothing of how she would feel having to share him. He had become so special to her, so much a part of her daily life.

The thought gave her an empty feeling that she couldn't shake. When it came right down to it, she didn't know if it was possible for her to keep her heart so coolly in check.

But it was the memory of the end of the evening that disconcerted her the most: the expression she had caught on John's face as he watched her and Timmy at the piano, the look in his eyes, and the odd huskiness in his voice when he'd said good night.

She had not expected the feelings that suddenly sprang into her heart—or that lingered still—the kind of feelings that were attached to dreams of hope and possibility.

She dared not have such dreams.

Clayton's face wavered before her eyes in an amorphous cloud. Through the months, his image had grown dimmer, until he was little more than a vague specter that she shoved into the farthest reaches of her mind.

Oh, if Clayton had only been the kind of husband who loved his wife, as John had loved his.

❧

Monday afternoon the garden club ladies were lined up at Mary's gate on the dot of three in their most fashionable gowns; wide-brimmed, flowered, and beribboned hats; and white gloves. They twittered up the blossom-banked walk of the lemon yellow, white-trimmed Queen Anne cottage like a flock of bonneted goslings. Their heads bobbing and turning, their bright eyes darting as they discovered the imported birdbath under the elm and the antique wrought iron and blown-glass hummingbird feeder tucked among the climbing roses by the front window.

Mary greeted them at the door, Timmy by her side in his

brand-new sailor suit, still creased from the box, that John had ordered from the Sears & Roebuck catalog just for the occasion. . .and his shiny new black shoes.

Mary had been affected and also impressed by John's forethought.

Though the ladies were generous in their compliments about her garden, it was clear, as she had suspected, that they had really come to finally get a look inside Mrs. Armitage's cottage. They clustered in groups in the living room, commenting on the wallpaper, the fabric on the settee and matching wingback chair; they admired the collection of miniature inlaid boxes on the table in the entry and the small landscape by Frederic Edwin Church on the library wall.

In the dining room, Mary observed more than one matron checking the hallmark on the china with a surreptitious flip of a saucer, as Bertha Warner had done that first day.

She felt more like a museum curator than a homeowner as she listened politely to extravagant compliments over the elegant linens and engraved sterling-silver tea service. In actuality the art and furnishings were worth more than she'd paid for the entire house.

Still, Mary had grown up in surroundings far more elegant and with possessions much more precious than these. But instead of being half amused by her guests' naive exuberance, as she had expected, she found herself delighted and touched. She was grateful to discover that their interest seemed less crass curiosity than sincere appreciation.

By the day's end, she felt she had made new friends.

She did not delude herself, however, that much was due to Timmy's quiet charm and the stalwart and uncompromising love and support of her sweet friend, Jane, who had "set the record straight" when it needed to be.

❧

Jane wouldn't have dreamed of leaving before everything was in apple-pie order. She, Mavis Dodd, and even Eunice Figg, who insisted that no job should be too small for the president, rolled up their sleeves and stayed until the last dish was dried.

"This could very well become an annual event in your lovely home, Mary." Eunice Figg sniffed, not out of an ulterior motive, Jane could see, but out of honest admiration.

"The garden club is always welcome." Mary smiled.

"That's certainly the way you made us feel," Mavis said.

"You have demonstrated that you will make an excellent member." Eunice sniffed. "We are happy you consented to join our little group."

Jane gave Mary a smile and a wink.

"Well, I'll be on my way. His Honor the mayor has the carriage waiting," Eunice said. "Can we give you ladies a ride home?"

"I'd appreciate that," Mavis said.

"That's kind, but I'll be along in a bit," Jane said. "Mary and I have some things to talk over."

Waiting until His Honor's carriage had turned the corner at First Street, Jane—holding cute little feather-haired Nancy—Mary, and Timmy collapsed on the front steps.

"Now the fun begins," Jane said, bouncing Nancy in her lap.

"You mean it isn't fun to wear yourself to a frazzle?" Mary dropped her arm around Timmy's shoulders.

"In my opinion, the best time of a party is when all the guests have gone and you can gossip about them."

"You're not a gossip," Mary admonished.

"Don't be too sure." Jane went nose to nose with Nancy who grabbed a handful of her hair. "Ouch. . . Well, Mary Smith," she exclaimed, disengaging Nancy's tight little fist, "you have made your mark! The tea was a resounding success! And as for you, Mr. Timmy, you are a gentleman of the old school."

He smiled shyly.

Mary leaned over and gave the top of his curly dark head a kiss. "And my courage," Jane heard her whisper as Timmy snuggled closer and laid his head against her shoulder.

"Your courage?"

"I couldn't have done it without him. He knows that." Mary looked down fondly at the boy and turned to Jane. "Or you, Jane! How can I ever repay you for denuding your own beautiful garden?"

"You would have done the same; I have no doubt of that, dear friend. Besides, Timmy and his daddy did most of the work."

Though Jane wasn't about to admit it, even to Mary, her opportunity to form a closer bond with John Aubrey had made the sacrifice more than worth it.

"Still, I wish there was something special I could do for you," Mary said. "Like maybe making you a new frock? But I'm all thumbs when it comes to sewing." Absently she stroked Timmy's arm. "Of course, I could bake a cake." She smiled wryly. "But all I know how to make is oatmeal cookies."

"And very fine oatmeal cookies, they are." John Aubrey had sneaked up, and as he spoke, he tickled Timmy under his chin. "Well, was it a success?" He dropped down on the step next to Mary.

Jane was surprised at his exuberance. She'd never seen him that way before. "I must say you're in good spirits."

"I figured there'd be leftovers."

The warm smile that he bestowed on her friend was not lost on Jane.

"You'd have been proud of your son," Mary said. "He received enough compliments to swell any small boy's head."

"That's because he knows enough to keep his mouth shut," John replied lightly, reaching across Mary to ruffle his son's hair.

Jane sat two steps above them, watching the exchange with a sinking heart. She hoped she was wrong. She prayed she was misreading the expression she imagined in John's eyes when he looked at her friend.

"You seem none the worse for wear, Miss Sheriff Jane," he said, smiling up at her with that heart-stopping smile of his.

"Is that supposed to be a compliment, sir?" Jane said in mock indignation.

He laughed.

That laugh was sound enough to get her heart pumping and moisture dimpling her brow.

"What I meant to say is," he continued, "after riding posse Saturday, you clean up very prettily."

"That's better." She turned Nancy around, face outward, holding the squirming body in a bear hug, resting her chin atop the baby's dark curls.

"Did you catch the robbers?" John asked.

"Oh, Jane, forgive me." Mary looked up. "I forgot to find out what happened."

Even Timmy sat up and took notice.

"We captured two of them," Jane said. "It was all very exciting. Unfortunately one got away."

"At least that should curtail their activities," John said.

"I expect so. The gang was getting too close for comfort."

"Were you afraid, Janie?" Mary asked.

"Not at first. I was just excited. I didn't think about being scared. When we picked up their trail, though, the unpleasant possibilities began to dawn on me, and my heart did begin to beat faster." She pursed her lips. "The closer we got to them, the faster it beat."

John leaned forward. "Where did you find them?"

"It was dusk by then," Jane said, warming to his attention. "We were near Logan's Pass. We got off our horses. . . ."

Jane lowered her voice, peril spilling into each inflection. She wasn't about to lose this moment of drama.

"Quietly we moved forward. We could hear voices behind the boulders. We reckoned they'd stopped to water their horses, and from their conversation, it was clear they thought they'd lost us and were deciding whether or not to hunker down there for the night."

"What happened then?" Mary whispered.

Jane squeezed Nancy closer against her, her voice tense with remembering.

"We left the horses and Sheriff Chisolm—he was heading up the posse—he gestured for some of us to climb around on the boulders to the right, a couple to the left, and he and Jason Bullock clambered up to the top of the ridge where he could overlook the stream. There were about eight of us altogether."

"I like the odds," John murmured.

Jane let out a deep sigh. "I could see Sheriff Chisolm. He had just reached the top. We were all waiting for his signal. I can tell you honestly, about then I was hardly breathing. Just at that moment, one of the horses that was drinking at the stream raised its head, looked around, and whinnied."

Jane paused. She had her audience in the palm of her hand. "You're surrounded," she shouted suddenly, imitating the sheriff.

Timmy jumped.

"Did the robbers shoot at you?"

"I'm still here, aren't I?" She cocked her head.

"But they went for their guns," John said.

"Well, no. As a matter of fact, when they saw eight rifles pointed between their eyes, their hands shot up like jackrabbits jumping out of a hole. They were bad but not stupid." Jane laughed. "I don't know if I *could* have pulled the trigger my hands were shaking so much." She looked rueful. "I've never shot a man. It's not high on my list of druthers."

Mary collapsed against the stair rail. "Oh my goodness." Then she began to giggle. "I guess our sheriff Janie is more for cajoling criminals into giving up their guns."

"I doubt that would have worked for that pair," John said.

"I reckon you're right," Jane said. "Fortunately that's not the kind of crime that comes often to Whispering Bluff. In fact, when my daddy was sheriff, I can only think of three times that he even had to pull his pistol, and that was only as a warning. Twice it wasn't even loaded."

John grinned. "So much for law enforcement in Whispering Bluff."

"I hope it stays that way. At least during my duty." Jane nuzzled Nancy's curls. "Don't you agree, sweetheart?"

Across Mulberry Street, where the fields began, the sun had dropped, now barely gilding the tops of the cornstalks.

Nancy began to fuss. "Oh dear, I guess I'm losing my charm."

"Never, Miss Sheriff," the new John teased.

That was promising.

"It's not you, Janie dear; it's past her feeding time," Mary said, rising. She reached for her daughter. "Come along, Mommy's darling."

With that John and Jane got up, too.

"I guess we should be going," he said.

Was that reluctance in his voice?

"Not before I give you some of those leftovers you came all this way for," Mary enjoined, starting up the steps. "I don't know what I'm going to do with all those cookies. Do you, Timmy?"

He rubbed his tummy and licked his lips.

"You take some, too, Sheriff. You can pass them out to your own special guests." Mary giggled and turned to John. "Rumor has it that the crime rate rises at dinnertime in the streets of Whispering Bluff."

"I've heard that rumor, too," John said. "In fact, there've been times Timmy and I thought we'd get ourselves arrested, just to have one of Sheriff Jane's famous dinners. I understand it even includes dessert."

"You don't have to get arrested for me to cook for you, John Aubrey," Jane said lightly but meant it from the depths of her heart. She brushed the back of her blue linen skirt. "Anyway,

I made a couple of chicken casseroles. One for Mary because I knew she'd be too tired to cook tonight and one for the two bachelors." She smiled at Timmy and then at John.

"Oh, Janie, you shouldn't. After all you've done. I'm embarrassed." Mary smiled. "And very, very grateful!"

"Timmy and I thank you, Miss Jane. I'm glad I don't have to rob a bank to get your attention."

You don't have to do anything but stand there. "My pleasure."

"Oh, I almost forgot," Mary said. "When did you decide to have Timmy's birthday party, John?"

"Saturday."

"Perfect! We're going to have a big celebration, and you, Jane, are at the top of the guest list. Isn't that so, Timmy?"

Timmy grinned and nodded.

"Mary offered to give him a party." The smile John gave Mary was warm and more than neighborly.

Couldn't Mary see what was so obvious?

Crushed, Jane picked up her bonnet. "Well, I must be off. I don't want to be cutting through the woods after dark."

"And you will not," John pronounced. "Before dark or any other time. Timmy and I are driving you home, Miss Sheriff Jane." He gave her a chagrined smile. "If you don't mind riding in a buckboard."

Jane curtsied. "I would be honored and most grateful to ride with you in whatever the conveyance."

He had no idea how true that was.

"In that case. . ." He offered her his arm.

Walking through the twilight toward John's house, Jane's spirits lifted. She couldn't blame him for being enamored of her friend. Who wouldn't be? Mary was so lovely and so good to Timmy. But time was on Jane's side. Mary was a married woman. It would not be long before he saw the hopelessness of his infatuation, and Jane would be there, his confidant and friend, always his willing companion.

"It's kind of you to give me a ride home, John. I must admit

I am a bit weary."

"Always my pleasure, Janie." John smiled down at her and patted her hand.

Yes, time was on her side.

sixteen

When John and Timmy returned from taking Jane home, Mary was waiting at the back steps with Jane's chicken casserole and a basket over her arm filled with leftover desserts.

"For your supper," she said, handing them to him. "When you have a chance, I have something I want to discuss with you about Timmy's party."

"Let me get him fed and to bed, and I'll be over."

An hour later, he knocked on Mary's back door and she came out, wrapping a light shawl around her shoulders.

The stars seemed close enough to touch, and the moon was bright and almost full, lighting the garden and her back stoop in an overlay of silver.

She settled on the top step, John on the one below.

"So, what did you have in mind?" he asked. "Not that one needs a reason to enjoy your company."

"I've been giving some thought to Timmy's birthday." She leaned forward. "Mavis reminded me this afternoon at the tea about the puppies she's looking to find homes for. It had occurred to me that one would be a perfect present. Timmy's just the right age, and it would be such good training."

"For the puppy or the boy?"

Mary laughed. "For the father."

"That's what I was afraid of."

"And since you have no flower beds to dig in, I see no impediment."

John was silent. "I've already gotten him a present, Mary. I bought him a model train. With all the cars and the tracks and—"

"But a boy needs a dog, John. And it should come from you."

"So should a train."

"Can't you give him two presents?"

John was annoyed. He knew she only had the best of intentions. But he'd planned the train as a special gift, one that Timmy would always remember, like John remembered his own fifth birthday when his dad had given him one.

The train was long gone, but he still had the memory of that birthday and the look of pleasure on his dad's face when John opened the box. John had always vowed he would bring up his son with the same wealth of love and memories.

How far the fruit had fallen from the tree of late.

And now his spirit was beginning to return. He was starting to get his bearings. Finally he was once again able to experience the joy of being a father, and Mary had barged in with her good intentions, *insisting* that she knew better.

He felt as if he'd been dashed with a dose of ice water.

"What is it?" Mary was looking at him quizzically.

"It's not that I don't want Timmy to have a dog," John said, "but I'd hoped this was the birthday he'd remember for the train. It just seems our family tradition would take second fiddle to a new puppy jumping all over him and licking his face."

It took Mary a minute to respond. When she did, she sounded chagrined. "I'm sorry, John. I didn't understand."

She looked so distressed his irritation dissolved at once, and all he wanted to do was reassure her. "Why would you understand? I certainly haven't been the great communicator."

"But still, I shouldn't have been so emphatic. I had no right."

"Of course you did."

"I didn't," she insisted.

"Mary, you did. I've been giving you the right for some time now."

He rose abruptly and walked down the steps. Facing away

toward the woods, he was silent for several minutes.

"It's time I was honest with you." He turned. Leaning back against the stair rail, he crossed his arms, and staring out toward the mulberry trees, he said, "Timmy didn't come over here all the time by chance. I encouraged him. I intentionally set out to make you his surrogate mother." He looked up at her. "Does that surprise you?"

He didn't wait for an answer. "You were the perfect choice. You were kind and compassionate, you had a wonderful way with him, and obviously he adored you. You were able to give him everything I could not." He took a deep breath. "And, you were married! Which meant I was absolved from any emotional responsibility toward you. What could have been more perfect?"

Now perfect has turned and bitten me in the heart. "So you see, you need make no apologies to me about having a right."

"Thank you for your honesty, John." Mary's voice was crisp. "But please, give me some credit. Don't you think I was smart enough to know what you were doing?" She clasped her hands in her lap. "Now, if I also may be honest, I did not have to accept the responsibility. But I did accept it, knowing full well your intentions. In fact, I welcomed it! Timmy was a gift to me—is a gift to me. We've all benefited. It doesn't matter the reasons. So you see, John, you may set your conscience at rest." She studied her clasped hands. "What saddens me is the note of regret I hear in your voice."

"Regret?" John mounted the stairs and again dropped onto the step below her. "Not for a minute. Not for a second. I'm only sorry that I wasn't honest with you from the beginning." He met her gaze and held it. "But I will never regret encouraging the relationship. Not for as long as I live."

A silence fell between them that lingered until he looked away. "In fact, Joanna would have probably said the Lord had a hand in it," he murmured.

"Joanna?"

"My wife. Joanna had a childlike faith in God's will."

"And you don't?"

"I'm afraid it's not always that simple for me." He smiled up at her. "But in this case, maybe she would have been right."

"I'd like to think so," Mary said quietly. "What was she like, John? Your wife."

He hadn't talked about Joanna in a long time. In fact, he was bemused that he had brought up her name now. For so long, he'd kept his silence. It had seemed the only way to keep his sanity.

"If it makes you uncomfortable. . ."

It surprised him that it did not. He felt himself quite willing to confide in this woman, Mary Smith. There was something about her, something in her demeanor that made him feel she would understand and not judge him too harshly.

"I don't mind," he said. "Joanna was small, like you. Her hair was brown. She had large, soft brown eyes. She was sweet, very sweet and gentle. . .and innocent. She was very close to her family in St. Louis, where we lived. I was a manager in her father's leather-goods factory."

"Quite a far cry from being a schoolmaster," Mary observed.

"He was grooming me to take over the business. He had no sons, and Joanna was his only child."

"It sounds like a wonderful opportunity." Mary cocked her elbow and rested her chin on her palm.

"Running a leather factory was the last thing I wanted to do with my life. At the time, I fancied myself a poet. After a couple of my plays were produced with some modest recognition—"

"I didn't know you were a playwright."

He smiled at her. "I imagine there's a lot we don't know about each other, Mary."

That seemed to fluster her. "I'm sorry," she said hastily. "I interrupted."

He continued. "Well, I decided if I was going to succeed at my so-called art it was about time I took it seriously. When my friend told me they were looking for a schoolmaster in Whispering Bluff, I saw my chance. I could support my family and still have time to write.

"Of course Joanna didn't share my enthusiasm. Her father had convinced her I was just an impractical dreamer. And she was timid; her world was small. She wasn't like you, Mary, capable and independent. I suspect you would have welcomed the challenge."

"Don't give me undue credit, John. One never knows what one would do under certain circumstances," Mary said softly.

"For Joanna, it was like pulling a fragile flower up by its roots. It was to my advantage that she believed in what the Bible has to say on the matter: 'What therefore God hath joined together, let not man put asunder.'"

"She was very brave," Mary murmured.

He paused. He'd never thought of Joanna as brave. He'd thought of her as needy, totally dependent, unable to reach out on her own. And yet, fearful as she was, she had taken that journey with him. Only because of him.

"Yes. Yes, she was brave."

"She must have loved you very much."

He could only nod.

Mary leaned forward, her face reflecting such compassion, looking at him with such avid concern, such unwavering focus that he suddenly found himself encouraged to confide more of those pent-up memories that had shackled his heart for so long.

Poised on the step above him, she became the vessel into which he poured the painful story of his journey: the slow trek across the plains, like pilgrims into the promised land, surmounting the rigors of a trip for which he and Joanna were so ill prepared. And finally recounting that last night in vivid detail: how they'd stopped by the road and set up camp; how he and Timmy had gone down to the stream, the sound of water burbling over the stones and the rustle of the aspen leaves; then the shrieks; Joanna, a living torch; how he'd struggled up the muddy hill; and how Timmy had screamed and screamed.

"Those were the last sounds he uttered."

Mary reached out and touched his shoulder but had the wisdom to remain silent.

"It's a guilt I'll live with the rest of my life," he muttered finally.

"That's a heavy burden to carry alone, John."

"Please, no religious platitudes, Mary," he said not unkindly, lifting his head.

"I wouldn't think of it." Her smile was gentle but a little sad.

"I don't deny God, Mary, if that's what you mean. But we do have to take responsibility for our own actions."

"But not necessarily the blame for their outcome."

"What's the difference?"

"We can't always control it—the outcome, that is. Sometimes other forces come into play. . .other people, whose motives are in conflict with our own. Even with God's. So don't be too hard on yourself, John. I'm sure God isn't."

"It would be a comfort to believe that."

"Then be comforted." She looked out toward the woods. "We all need comfort, John. And it's there for us if we can accept it."

"You're a wise woman, Mary."

"Not so wise. Sometimes it's easier to give advice than to take it."

"Nevertheless. . ." He pushed himself up from the steps and gazed down at her.

She was so beautiful, so pale and lovely, so fragile in the moonlight. And yet he knew that beneath the apparent fragility was a strong, passionate, independent spirit. Mary Smith was a competent woman who was nevertheless capable of deep compassion and tenderness, as he'd witnessed with his son, Timmy.

The duality of her nature intrigued and attracted him in a

way that he'd never experienced before.

As he looked down at her now, she quite literally took his breath away.

Suddenly stunned at the direction his thoughts were taking, he turned abruptly. "I'd probably better go home before Timmy has another one of his night walks."

"Oh my. Indeed you should. Where has the time gone?"

He reached down to help her up. "Though I'm not too worried. He hasn't had one of those episodes since you came into his life."

She was standing now and quite steady. Still, he couldn't seem to make himself release her.

Foolish, foolish, he thought, as the smooth softness of her small white hand engaged his senses.

"You've been a good friend, Mary," he said gruffly. "Your—your husband is a lucky man."

He shouldn't have said that, either. He knew it, but the words just came out.

And she didn't withdraw her hand. Not immediately.

As he trudged home, he reflected on the expression that had fallen across her face when he'd mentioned her husband and the deep luminosity of her eyes that he wanted to fathom but could not.

seventeen

Last night had given Mary an insight into John Aubrey that she wasn't sure she welcomed.

She understood him better now, the reasons for his guilt and sadness and his self-imposed isolation. She also realized how easily she, herself, could be sucked into the maelstrom of the conflicting currents of his passionate nature. For there they lurked, churning beneath his reticence and brooding wistfulness.

As she went about her tasks that day, thoughts of him kept intruding. Even now, as she sat at the piano aimlessly chording snatches of a song here, bits of a sonata there, she was unable to suppress them.

Timmy's timorous knock at the front door managed finally to divert her.

"Come in, dear."

She could hear the squeal of the hinges and cautious closing. She almost would have welcomed a loud, normal slam.

He was so timid.

He slipped through the front hall and skittered up beside her at the piano, leaning against her like a small kitten seeking to be stroked. She turned, planting a kiss on the tip of his ear. He smelled of boy and licorice.

"Your daddy and you took a detour by Thompson's on the way home from school, I'd wager."

He stared at her.

"How do I know, you ask? Magic powers!" She played a dark chord with her left hand and smiled at him, pushing her nose close to his face. "I can smell it on your breath."

He grinned and reached into the pocket of his coveralls,

pulling out a small bag and offering it to her.

"Ah, my favorite," she said, selecting a black button of the candy and popping it into her mouth. "Thank you very much."

As he had two nights before, Timmy watched transfixed while she allowed her fingers to play over the keys in various themes and variations.

"Did you hear a familiar tune?" she asked.

He nodded, smiling broadly. Then, to her utter amazement, he lifted his right hand to the keyboard and picked out the melody of "Twinkle, Twinkle, Little Star."

"Timmy! Do my eyes deceive me? Play that again."

He did.

"You are playing the piano!" she said, her breath catching. Her heart was beating so fast it hurt. "That's amazing! Does your daddy know you can do that?"

He shook his head.

For a moment, she could only gaze at him in incredulous silence. Then she said, "I have an idea. Your birthday is coming up. Wouldn't that be a fine present to give him? To hear you play the piano."

She folded her hands in her lap. "When two people play at the same time, it's called a duet. You and I are going to play a duet for your daddy. Now, you play 'Twinkle, Twinkle, Little Star' again, like you just did, and let's see what happens."

As Timmy played the melody with his right hand, Mary added a simple chorded harmony with her left. When they had finished, she lifted him up onto her lap and whirled around on the piano stool. "What did you think of that?" she cried, coming to a breathless stop.

Quivering with excitement, he climbed down from her lap, and with eyes shining, he grabbed her hand and placed it again on the keyboard.

"You want to play it again?"

He nodded. Then, his little foot tapping out the beat, he

glanced at her and began.

Over and over, they played "Twinkle, Twinkle, Little Star." They played it quick and slow, soft and loud, silly and serious. Joyfully! Laughing! To Mary it sounded like the music of the angels.

A howl from upstairs brought her suddenly down to earth.

Conscience-stricken, she jumped up. "I won't be a minute, Timmy. You keep practicing while I'm gone."

She found Nancy sitting up in her crib, looking woefully abandoned, tears streaming down her round, mottled little face, her bib soaked, her dark curls tangled.

"I am so sorry, darling," Mary said, sweeping the baby up into her arms. "Did you think Mommy had forgotten you?" She covered Nancy's wet apple cheeks with guilty kisses.

In short order, she had changed her. "Mommy's going to make you all pretty," she said and pulled a pink gingham pinafore out of the drawer. "That should make you feel better," she declared, pulling it over Nancy's head.

She was just beginning to tie a matching ribbon around the baby's topknot curl, when suddenly "Twinkle, Twinkle, Little Star" floated up from downstairs—melody and chords!

She froze.

Was that possible?

She cocked her head, listening. Not trusting what she heard.

Grabbing Nancy up, she ran down the stairs.

At the living room entry, she stopped short.

She stood with her mouth agape.

Tears welled in her eyes.

Timmy sat perched on the piano stool, his little legs dangling. With his right hand, he played the melody, with his left, the chords, just as she had played them.

A wavering little voice sang along, " 'Twinkle, twinkle, little star, how I wonder what you are! Up above the world so high, like a diamond in the sky. Twinkle, twinkle, little star, how I wonder what you are!'"

She'd always known Timmy was gifted, the way he could read and do his numbers at so young an age. But now she saw that "gifted" was an understatement.

Behind that small, serious facade was the talent, the intelligence, the soul of a truly brilliant child.

All he'd needed was the opportunity and nurturing love to bloom, just as her garden had. Only brighter, so very much brighter.

Once Timmy had discovered that he could play the piano, there was no stopping him. Every day, as soon as he and John returned home from school, he was at her door.

"I'm beginning to feel a bit guilty," John said one day in passing. "I hope he isn't bothering you."

"Quite the contrary," Mary assured him. "I look forward to his visits, and he amuses Nancy."

Which was quite the truth. While Mary and Timmy practiced, Nancy sat in her high chair by the piano and, bouncing up and down, beat out her own rhythm with a wooden spoon.

Mary could hardly believe the joy she felt watching Timmy's tousled dark curls as he bent over the keyboard, his little fingers dancing on the keys each day with firmer conviction, his sweet voice growing stronger as he diligently practiced "Twinkle, Twinkle, Little Star," the birthday surprise for his father.

It was touching. It was thrilling.

But although he didn't hesitate to sing, he was still reticent to speak, even to her.

She was amazed at how easily he had picked up the melodies of some of the old familiar hymns and, with her help, even learned simple chord accompaniments.

All this reinforced her certainty of the child's amazing and unusual musical gift.

One warm afternoon, when the scented spring breezes blew through her open windows and she was feeling especially frivolous and joyful, she taught Timmy a lively rendition of "Pop Goes the Weasel," which they both sang with exuberant gusto, encouraged by Nancy's lively poundings and tinkling laughter.

Every time they came to the "Pop," Timmy would jump off the stool and Nancy would bang her spoon on the tray of her high chair with a resounding smack that sent them all into gales of laughter, prompting Timmy to insist that they play it over and over with increasing speed and glee.

In the midst of the hilarity, she glanced out toward the garden and, to her dismay, saw John standing on the steps of his house—facing hers.

She caught Timmy's hands and covered his mouth, nodding toward the window.

Timmy's round brown eyes stared up into hers. He jumped off the stool with a thud and ran to the window, just as John began his determined stride toward Mary's cottage.

Quivering with concern, he peeked out over the sill.

John's heard us, Mary thought. *He's heard us, and now Timmy's birthday surprise will be ruined.*

She rushed to Timmy's side, and with her finger to her lips, she shook her head, urging him gently back to the piano, where she sat him on her lap and began to play "Pop Goes the Weasel," only now alone and with embellishments.

The door knocker clacked, but Mary continued playing, as if she didn't hear it.

Again it banged.

This time she paused, crinkling her nose at Timmy, who sat squirming nervously in her lap.

The third time, she called, "Yes? Who is it?"

As if they didn't know.

"It's I, Mary, John," came the voice from without.

"Oh. It's you, John. I wasn't sure." *Oops, a small lie.* She'd have to deal with that later.

Mary disengaged Timmy and set him on the floor; then she rose and walked sedately to the front door. She winked at Timmy, to set him at ease, and opened it.

There John stood, dark suited and serious and handsome enough to steal any maiden's heart—provided the maiden's heart was available.

"I didn't realize you were having company this afternoon," he said.

"Company?" She gave him a questioning look. "Other than Timmy?"

"I heard two voices."

Mary began to laugh merrily. "Well I certainly had you fooled. 'Tis only me. I was entertaining the children with my silliness."

John frowned. "I could have sworn—"

"Not in front of the child," she said playfully, covering Timmy's ears.

Still, John hesitated, as if he were not wholly convinced.

"Come and see for yourself," she said, standing aside. "It's only Timmy and me. . .and Nancy, of course. Or is this just your excuse to join us for a glass of lemonade?"

John remained in the threshold. "Thank you. A rain check. I think Timmy'd better come along with me, anyway. I don't want him to outstay his welcome, and I have to go back to school. I forgot a book I need for a test I'm giving tomorrow."

Timmy's hand tightened around hers.

"Can't he stay awhile longer?" she pleaded. "We're having such a good time."

John glanced down at Timmy who was nodding so vigorously he looked like one of those dolls whose head was attached to a spring.

"I can see where his heart lies," John said, flashing a fine smile.

Timmy snuggled up against her skirt, leaving no doubt.

"Then he may stay?" Mary returned John's smile.

"Very well." John turned and bounded down the steps. "I'll be back before dark."

"Maybe you can join us for supper," she called after him.

"I'll think about it." Suddenly he swung around, the girl-swooning grin still lighting his face. "There! I've thought about it. Supper it is. Since you insist."

A little bubble of excitement sprang in Mary's breast. "That will be nice," she murmured.

She watched until he disappeared around the corner of the cottage, quietly closed the door, and leaned back against it—then realized she'd not only deceived John but did it in front of his impressionable son.

Well, it hadn't been a total lie. She *had* been entertaining the children.

But she couldn't deny it. Misleading distortion seemed to be coming too easily to her lips, and certainly it was a bad example for Timmy.

He was looking up at her with a relieved grin on his handsome little face. . .so much the image of his father's.

A very bad example! Very bad, indeed!

She squatted beside him, taking both his little hands in hers and gazing into his eyes with serious consideration. "I don't want you to think it's a good idea to make up stories, Timmy. It is *never* right to deceive someone. However. . .this may be the one exception, when a lovely surprise is in the offing. And when we know the whole truth will soon come out."

His face was so solemn, his eyes round and trusting, listening to her as he always did, listening to every word with such utmost confidence and trust.

What a responsibility that was.

She smiled at him, and he smiled back. Even at almost five, it was his father's smile: brown eyes crinkling at the corners, wide, generous mouth, and sparkling teeth.

She hugged him to her, imagining that same smile on John's face when he saw, for the first time, the amazing performance of his extraordinary child.

Maybe. . .oh please, dear God. . .maybe that moment will help to put their tragic past to rest.

The birthday picnic was under the oak out in back. There were ham and cheese sandwiches, Jane's cucumber pickles, fruit and fresh lemonade, and, of course, Jane's famous chocolate cake. Hitch took charge of the homemade ice cream.

Displaying almost no shyness, Timmy beamed through the whole celebration. These were folks he was used to and folks who cared so very much about him.

John's housekeeper, tall, rawboned Mrs. Grice, and Mary's plump little Mrs. Meade, with her gray flyaway knot, spent the afternoon chasing Nancy—a great blessing, now that she had begun crawling and getting into everything.

Even though there were no other little ones there, the grown-ups got into the spirit with enthusiastic games of tag and a competitive Pin the Tail on the Donkey.

And then it was time for the presents.

Jane had sewn Timmy a little deputy's shirt that she'd designed to match her own, with a fringe; and she also gave him a real star that she'd wrapped separately in silver paper.

Hitch brought him a child-sized hoe from Thompson's General Store, and Mavis Dodd had made what she called a "go-to-meeting outfit" of knickers and a matching jacket.

If that wasn't a hint to pull John back into the fold, Mary had never seen one.

Mrs. Grice and Mrs. Meade had teamed up to knit Timmy a little woolen cap and matching scarf for "when the weather got brisk," and Pru and Pastor Pike contributed a children's Bible, with Timmy's name inscribed inside.

No surprise there.

Mary had consulted Katherine Ainsworth, the town librarian, and chosen a book about animals and one about birds, both with colored illustrations, and another on the stars. She'd also purchased *Mutt, A Dog* because she hadn't yet given up on a puppy.

But of course, the hit of the day was John's train, with

the engine, caboose, Pullman, and boxcars in between, the full track, the station, and even little houses and trees and a bridge. He and Timmy set it up on the grass, and everyone had a go at playing with it.

Finally it was time to pack up, and they all lent a hand. The train was returned neatly to its crate; the dishes were gathered and carried into the kitchen, washed and dried before Mary had a chance to turn around.

"Before you go," she said, "I have one final surprise."

They all gathered in the parlor, crowding onto the settee, the Queen Anne chair and the pair of tufted ones across from it, and around the game table. They even pulled in chairs from the dining room.

John leaned against the jamb of the living room entry. Was it because there was no more room to sit or because he preferred to keep his distance? But now was not the time to study John. This was Timmy's day.

Mary waited until they were all settled and quiet, and then she said, "And now, Timmy has a gift for all of you."

With that, he stepped from behind her, and with a confidence that surprised even her, he lifted the cover on the piano keys and scrambled up onto the stool.

The room was still, as if they had all drawn one tense, collective breath.

Timmy took his time, as Mary had taught him. He sat for a moment, breathed deeply, then lifted his little hands to the keyboard. As he played, his sweet clear voice rang out, " 'Twinkle, twinkle, little star. . .'"

When he finished, there was a protracted silence.

He sat, for a moment, expecting the applause that Mary had promised.

Finally it came, echoing throughout the room. He scrambled down off the stool, gave a brief bow as she'd taught him, and, in a sudden fit of shyness, ran into his father's waiting arms, burying his face against his chest.

John held him close. "Oh, Timmy, I love you, son. I love you so much."

"I love you, too, Papa," came the muffled reply.

Standing beside him, Mary watched the montage of emotions play across John's face: the suffering, the guilt, the regret, and at last, at last, the poignant joy. It was all she could do not to reach out and comfort him.

But she couldn't; she dared not. So she held herself apart and turned away, engulfed in the pandemonium as everyone gathered around them.

"We need you in the children's choir," Pru Pike enthused, reaching him first, touching his arm, and putting her sweet face close to his.

For a moment, Mary was afraid he would shrink from shyness, but instead, he smiled.

Hitch ruffled his hair. "Good job, partner!"

And Mavis Dodd, a widow, said, "If I find myself another husband, Timmy, you will definitely sing at my wedding."

Misses Grice and Meade hovered close, and Nancy pulled a lock of his hair that elicited a loud "*ouch*," which confirmed that Timmy had, indeed, found his voice.

Drained, Mary dropped onto the stool that Timmy had vacated.

What a day it has been!

What a week it has been!

She looked up to find John watching her.

The naked emotion in his eyes caught her off guard. For too long, she allowed her gaze to linger and felt the warmth of blood rising in her cheeks—and a breathless, throbbing ache in her heart.

Distressed by her reaction, she turned. . .and met Jane's pensive regard.

eighteen

Timmy insisted on dragging his treasure trove of presents in a single trip, when three would have made far more sense. He reminded John of a little jackrabbit bouncing about, his head bobbing as he bent to retrieve fallen items from his overflowing basket. John followed with amused impatience, balancing his own burden of the boxes that held Timmy's train.

And all the while, Timmy was chattering on about the day, his presents. . .and Miss Mary.

Miss Mary.

Mary.

The utter and profound joy that John felt in seeing his child transformed was shadowed by the conflicting feelings that he felt for this woman, Mary Smith. The swing of emotions at even the mention of her name—which Timmy did, over and over in unrelenting glee, almost as if to taunt him—was difficult to bear.

It couldn't be love. She was a married woman, after all.

Admiration, gratitude. Deep gratitude!

And attraction. He had to admit it. What red-blooded man in his right mind wouldn't find her attractive? The woman had everything. There was a pale, feminine beauty about her that was so compelling with her dark, curling hair, violet eyes much too large for her delicate, perfectly featured face with its turned-up nose, luscious lips, and slightly pointed chin, her small, exquisitely formed figure, and her voice like that of an angel.

Oh yes, not an inch of her had escaped him.

And yet for all her fragile beauty, she had a strong, passionate nature—he'd been the object of that. . .more than once. But she also had a humility about her—a gentleness, a compassion, a generosity, a sunny disposition and loving nature. . . .

What that woman lacked, no woman needed.

Yes, there was an attraction there. He could not deny it.

And when Timmy sat down at that piano and played and sang and said, "I love you, too, Papa," John was so grateful to her that he wanted to gather her up into his arms right along with his son. His feelings were that deep.

Not love. Gratitude.

It cannot, must not, be love.

How could he even be contemplating the merits of another woman, even one as remarkable, beautiful, and talented a woman as Mary Smith? How could he turn his back on all those years with Joanna who had adored him, depended on him, believed in him, sacrificed so much for him? Sacrificed her very life.

"Papa. Papa, are you listening to me?" Timmy was waiting at the back stairs, his little hand resting on the handle of the basket.

"I'm sorry; what did you say, son?"

What business had he, thinking about that woman when he should be concentrating on this miraculous, wonderful child of his?

"Papa, I want to go to church tomorrow. It's Sunday, and I want to sit with Miss Mary and Miss Jane and see Pastor Pike and Miss Pru and everybody else. They're all going to be there, Papa. They told me so."

It was a conspiracy.

"We'll talk about it when we get all these things in the house," John said, putting his foot on the first step.

"I want to talk about it now!" Timmy looked up defiantly, his hands on his hips.

"Feeling your oats, are you, young man?" All these months he'd waited for the boy to speak, and now he wouldn't keep his little mouth shut.

"I mean it, Papa. Everybody wants us there. They said so."

"I'll think about it."

"That means yes. That means yes. Yay!" Timmy grinned and began hauling the basket of tumbling toys up the stairs.

With a sigh, John deposited his boxes on the kitchen table and returned to retrieve it all, including his son, whom he picked up like a sack of meal, carrying the giggling boy over his shoulder into the house and depositing him with a thump on a kitchen chair.

Later, as he tucked a drowsy, happy Timmy into bed, he contemplated this miraculous day and the rebirth of his remarkable child.

And all because of Mary.

Married Mary.

He rolled his eyes heavenward. *Folks say You have a sense of humor, God, but must You make me the butt of Your joke?*

The next morning, John was tossed awake, literally, by an exuberant Timmy bouncing on his bed.

It was barely dawn.

"Time to get up, Papa. We've got to get ready for church."

John rubbed his eyes. Through a fitful night, he'd had second thoughts about going to church, strong second thoughts. And he'd come up with a plan—one that wouldn't disappoint Timmy and would get him off the hook.

"You know, son, your dad has a lot of work to do. Next week is the last week of school, and I have tests to prepare and compositions to correct and—"

Timmy stopped bouncing. Tears welled up in his eyes. "You mean we're not going to church?"

"I didn't say that. You are definitely going to church. But *I* am not." John pushed off the covers and gave Timmy an encouraging hug. "Right after breakfast, I'm going to go over and talk to Miss Mary. You can go with her. That's even better!"

Timmy didn't look so sure. "But I wanted to go with you, Papa."

Stay out of this, God! Stop spreading on the guilt!

"Another time. All right?"

Timmy's expression made it clear that it was not all right but better than not going at all.

"Now you go brush your teeth and wash your face and get dressed while I make breakfast." He turned the boy around and gave him a loving push toward the hall.

As John fried bacon and whipped up some eggs to scramble, his eyes, as always, were drawn like a magnet to the cottage across the way. Mary's cottage, abundant with a myriad of colors and textures and happy surprises like the new bird-bath in the middle of the front lawn and the stone mother duck and her ducklings, wandering through the side garden— reflections of the joyful humor and taste of the remarkable woman who lived there.

His eyes were ever drawn to it, as he was drawn to her.

As he mounted Mary's back steps a half hour later, he thought, *You were supposed to lead us out of temptation, Lord. But it seems all You do is push me toward it.*

He knocked on her kitchen door, anticipating some resistance when she heard his request, but knowing how she loved Timmy, he had no doubt of the outcome.

She answered almost immediately. "Why, John? It's so early." Her amethyst eyes widened in surprise as she modestly pulled her red kimono closer. "What's the matter? Is something wrong with Timmy?"

Her abundant dark hair still in a loose night braid draped over her shoulder in the most beguiling way.

John had to regain his breath before answering.

"Timmy's fine. But he wants to go to church."

"How wonderful."

"Unfortunately I'm not able to take him. . . ." John continued with the litany of excuses he'd already practiced on his son.

He could hear Nancy chortling in the background as Mary gazed at him in silence. Finally she said, "I'm sorry, John. I'm afraid I won't be able to. I have plans after church."

"But. . ." He was shocked. He couldn't believe that she was turning him down. "But he wants to go so much."

"It's only two hours out of a Sunday, John. I'm sure if you try, you can make the time." Just as the door was closing, she peeked out. "See you at church." And then it shut all the way, leaving him standing there with nothing to do but turn around and head for home.

John stalled until the very last minute before bringing chatty Timmy to church. Blessedly, when they arrived, there was no one outside. But as he hoisted Timmy down from the buckboard, he heard the music begin.

And so did Timmy.

"Papa, we're late!"

"Wait," John called as Timmy made a wild dash toward the double front doors of the little wooden church.

Too late!

He swung them wide and ran in, his new shoes smacking the floor in loud announcement.

By the time John entered the narthex, Timmy was already halfway to the front of the sanctuary. Cringing, he could do nothing but follow, down the center aisle, in full view of the whole congregation.

To his chagrin, Timmy made a beeline for Mary, who was holding Nancy and, of course, sitting in the second row next to Jane. Timmy sidled in front of the other worshipers, plopped down beside her, and snuggled close, leaving plenty of room so John could slide in beside him.

And to make matters worse, even before the announcements, Pastor Pike welcomed John Aubrey and his miracle son, Timmy. A twitter of response passed through the congregation, and folks down the row and across the aisle leaned forward with welcoming smiles to which he felt compelled to respond, as well as to the warm pats on his shoulder from those in the row behind.

Had he tried for their attention, he could not have been more successful.

It was after the announcements that the service took on a more serious tone, when Pastor Pike announced that Mavis Dodd's brother had been killed in a hunting accident and that Mavis had taken the early train to Denver to be with the family.

A ripple of sighs went through the sanctuary, for some, no doubt, had known him. And if not, they knew Mavis and obviously cared deeply for her.

The pastor continued. "As I prayed with Mavis last night and saw her off this morning, I was moved to set aside my sermon on the second chapter of James and address what is weighing on all our hearts as we keep her in our thoughts and prayers during this difficult time—the matter of death and dying."

John shot a glance at Timmy. *Of all Sundays to bring him to church, when the whole sermon would be focusing on death. The minute it gets too much for him, I'll whisk him out of here, no matter how bad it looks.*

"Please open your Bibles to First Thessalonians 4:13 and 14, and follow along."

There was a swish of turning pages, and Pastor Pike began to read. " 'I would not have you to be ignorant, brethren, concerning them which are asleep, that ye sorrow not, even as others which have no hope. For if we believe that Jesus died and rose again, even so them also which sleep in Jesus will God bring with him.'

"And now turn to Second Corinthians 5:7 and 8. 'For we walk by faith, not by sight: We are confident, I say, and willing rather to be absent from the body, and to be present with the Lord.'"

He laid his open hand on the Bible. "I suggest that we all

pray for that faith to believe, to believe that God has a purpose for each of us, in this life and in the next."

He continued with additional words of interpretation and inspiration, scriptures about the wonderful place God had prepared for each of His children, who often leave their families bereft, unable to understand why their loved ones have been taken.

John felt the words cutting into him. He hadn't thought about Joanna and the glorious place she'd gone—only selfishly about himself, wallowing in his own pain, his own unfilled needs.

The minister then asked the congregation to turn to Second Corinthians 1:3 and 4. " 'Blessed be God, even the Father of our Lord Jesus Christ, the Father of mercies, and the God of all comfort; who comforteth us in all our tribulation, that we may be able to comfort them which are in any trouble, by the comfort wherewith we ourselves are comforted of God.'

"When our dear Mavis returns," he concluded, "we must surround her with all the love and comfort of which the Bible speaks, as we, ourselves, in our time of trouble must be comforted."

Finally he concluded, " 'Blessed are they that mourn: for they shall be comforted.' Let us now bow our heads in prayer."

John glanced at Mary, remembering the night when he'd confided his own sadness and how she had reminded him then to be comforted.

He looked down at Timmy, beside him, nestled up against her, his little head bowed. Was it possible that this small soul instinctively understood more than John? He'd had the wisdom to allow, even welcome, Mary's embracing comfort.

How much time he, John, had wasted in anger and guilt, and how damaging it had been to both him and Timmy.

As he allowed his wandering gaze to follow his thoughts, he realized how his suffering and Timmy's had been multiplied by his inability or unwillingness—or arrogance—to open himself to the comfort that was, as Mary had reminded him, waiting for him, if only he was willing to accept it. How much easier it would have been had he joined this congregation of believers who would have so willingly and lovingly shared his grief and offered comfort.

But it was not too late.

As he bowed his head, he offered his own silent prayer. *Forgive me for blaming You, Lord, for Joanna's death. Help me to be grateful for the blessings You have provided here on earth and the glorious promise of the life to come. Let me overcome my fear and arrogance and look only to You for my guidance and inspiration.*

And as an afterthought...

And, Lord, I beg You, help me set my heart in the right direction, away from that which I should not covet.

Amen.

nineteen

She was a married woman. Or a murderess! And no matter how far she'd run from her despicable husband, that fact did not change. To have thoughts of another man, even in fantasies, even in dreams, was a biblical sin.

Mary knew that.

But it was so hard when the object of her forbidden fantasies and dreams was so close at hand, when she could hardly look out her window without glimpsing him.

And to make matters worse, now that Timmy had rediscovered his voice, there was no stopping the child, and all he seemed to want to talk about was his latest adventure with his father. To the point that at times, she felt a conspiracy against her heart, as if God were testing, even punishing her, not only with her own temptation but with the hollow recognition that her little Nancy would never know the love of such a father.

If the passage in James was true: "Blessed is the man that endureth temptation," she was certainly blessed.

But even as she endured her temptation, she made a point of avoiding it.

That was why, if she was in her garden and John appeared across the way, she hurried inside with little more than a perfunctory wave; why, when she encountered him in church—which she did each Sunday now that Timmy was in Pru's children's choir—she would not tarry but nod pleasantly and move on. She even took to arriving early at the Sunday service to avoid passing him on the way.

It was such a Sunday in late June when her phaeton broke an axle halfway between home and Good Shepherd Community Church.

Should she unhitch Queenie and go back for the buckboard? Or should she leave the mare and the rig where they were and go on? Either way, having to carry Nancy, she would surely be late. To make matters worse, Timmy was singing in this Sunday's service, and no matter what she did, she was afraid she'd miss hearing him.

She had just made up her mind to trudge on and take her chances—what other alternative had she?—when she heard a horse's whinny and a buckboard pulled to a stop beside her.

"You can't very well avoid me now."

Trembling in the wash of John's subdued baritone, she paused then turned.

There he sat gazing down at her, Timmy smiling innocently at his side.

"Hi, Miss Mary," Timmy squealed, moving over to make room for her.

"Hi, Timmy." She swallowed, struggling for equanimity. "I'm afraid I broke an axle," she said, not meeting John's eyes.

"So I see." He jumped down. "Timmy and I are never ones to miss an opportunity to come to the aid of a lady in distress," he said drily, circling the buckboard. "I'll deal with the rig after church."

"Thank you. I really appreciate it. Hitch is gone for a few days, visiting relatives."

Without asking, he took Nancy from her arms and helped Mary up beside Timmy then handed the baby back to her.

"Thank you," she managed as he hopped nimbly into the wagon on the other side and picked up the reins.

Mary smiled down at Timmy. "I'm looking forward to hearing you sing in church this morning," she said as the horse started to move.

"I'm singing with the big choir."

"I know, Miss Pru told me. 'All Things Bright and Beautiful.' It's one of my favorites."

Bouncing up and down on the seat, Timmy began to practice

in his clear, sweet voice. " 'Each little flower that opens, each little bird that sings, He made their glowing colors, He made their tiny wings.' "

He lifted his thin arms as if he were conducting, urging Mary and John to join in the chorus, which they did, their tension momentarily eased as they smiled at each other over his bobbing head.

" 'All things bright and beautiful, all creatures great and small, all things wise and wonderful: The Lord God made them all.' "

Suddenly tears welled up in Mary's eyes. It was all so natural, so warm and loving, this closeness.

So unattainable.

Timmy continued, bouncing along to the rhythm, singing each verse, conducting them in the chorus. But now Mary carefully averted her eyes from John's and gazed ahead of her to where the white church steeple peeked above the trees, and she blinked back the threatening tears.

"Why, Mary?" John asked quietly.

She had to look at him then, acknowledge that he had spoken. "Why what?"

"Why have you been avoiding me? What have I done to offend you?"

"Is that the way it seems?"

He gave a wry laugh. "For the last two weeks, all you've shown me is the back of your head." He held her gaze, locked it in, unwilling to release it until he got an answer.

Mary's heart pounded. She could hardly bear the troubled longing in his eyes, a longing that she mirrored in her own heart but dared not let him see.

Oh how she yearned to respond, to satisfy that need that bound them both.

"Blessed is the man that endureth temptation. . . ." But only if I had the strength to resist it.

"John, I. . ."

"Don't look away!"

She pulled Nancy closer and took a deep breath. "Some—sometimes it's better if things aren't put into words. That way they don't really exist."

"You think that's so?"

"I think it has to be."

"Papa." Timmy yanked on his father's sleeve. "Clyde's stopped. We're going to be late for church."

"Sorry, son." John dragged his gaze from Mary's and set his eyes on the road. He snapped the reins, and the long-legged roan resumed his trot.

At the church, John tethered Clyde to the hitching post at the side of the little wooden sanctuary then hoisted Timmy down from the buckboard. As Timmy ran off, he reached for Nancy and helped Mary alight.

Their eyes met.

"Mary…"

"Please, John," she murmured, lowering her gaze. "Don't make it any harder."

Next to them, Leonard Figg heaved his considerable bulk out of his stylish buggy, having deposited his wife, Eunice, by the front door. "Morning, schoolmaster. Beautiful day."

"Good morning, Your Honor."

"Ah, I see you're being a good neighbor," he said, catching sight of Mary.

"A good *Samaritan*," Mary hastily corrected. She wanted there to be no doubt. "My carriage broke down. You'll find it in the middle of Mayberry Street."

"Either way, sir, you're doing God's work." The mayor waved as he joined his wife on the steps.

Ushering Mary into the cool, flower-scented narthex of the simple little church, John murmured, "I hope you don't mind if we take a detour home. Jane's on duty and couldn't make it to church, so Timmy promised to give her a private concert."

Mary nodded. "Of course."

If only John would switch his attention to Jane. Life would be so much less complicated.

twenty

Jane's desk was in the front window of the sheriff's office where she could look out across Main, kitty-corner to the bank and all the way up the north side of the street to the feed store. It gave her a pretty good idea of what was going on in town most of the time.

She glanced up at the clock above the telegraph machine.

Church would be just getting out—provided Pastor Pike's sermon didn't run over—and folks would be lining up to shake his hand. That would take about fifteen or twenty minutes as the pastor was one to give each parishioner a due share of his attention then a few minutes to chat on the front steps.

It would be a good half hour before John and Timmy arrived.

And for once, Mary would not be there to serve as a distraction.

She loved Mary and knew she had done nothing to encourage John's attention. But the attraction was there—and clear to Jane. Be that as it was, she also knew that John was too fine and moral a gentleman to pursue a married lady. So she would continue her quest, trusting that in time, one day she would be able to engage his heart.

She smoothed her buckskin skirt for the umpteenth time, shaking out the fringe at the hem, even though it was perfectly straight. She adjusted the matching vest, on which she had so meticulously embroidered tiny red, white, and blue stars.

It was a special outfit that she had made to wear at parades and inaugural ceremonies and when greeting visiting dignitaries—should there ever be any. Even though John did

149

not fit in any of those categories, she had decided to wear it anyway.

Besides, it was Sunday!

She glanced around the office, puffing up a fringed pillow, adjusting the straight-back chair next to her desk, straightening a watercolor above the credenza.

It had been a bare, no-nonsense office before Jane became sheriff. But she had made it her own. She strongly believed that everyone benefited from being surrounded by beauty, no less so the violators. Perhaps they needed beauty even more! It was her contention that it would inspire them to better ways. She hung paintings by local artists in her office and in the hall, where they were visible to the jail cells, and covered the bunks with patchwork quilts stitched by the sewing guild of which she was a founding member. Sometimes she even played her residents (she shrank from calling them inmates or convicts) classical music on the gramophone because she'd read that "Music hath charms to soothe the savage beast."

Speaking of which, she could hear Skubby Walker's snoring from the last cell at the end of the hall. Sleeping it off from Saturday night. Which reminded her that she must send a food package to his wife, Maude, and the five little young ones—poor urchins.

She adjusted the roses in the cut glass vase on her desk.

Outside only a couple of carriages passed: Doc Warner and Bertha then Mavis. She waved. Most folks went home by way of First Street instead of Main.

She glanced again at the clock. It wouldn't be long now.

Peter Chaloupek rode by with Becca's dad, Jacob Hostettler, in the seat next to him.

Jane returned their wave.

Becca was still in Boulder. It was a testament to the strength of her and Peter's young marriage that they could be separated for so long while she finished medical school. But soon she'd be home for good; then she'd be the one sitting next to Peter in the buggy and her daddy would be riding in back—and real happy about it. Jane knew Jacob missed Becca almost as much as Peter did, if that was possible.

It hadn't been easy losing Peter to her best friend. Deep down she'd always known Becca was first in his heart. But when she took up with that fancy Fullrider fellow, whose family's name was on all the important buildings in Boulder, Peter had turned to Jane.

Becca came to her senses just in time and realized where she belonged and with whom, and that put an end to Jane's dreams. Even though it hurt at the time, in her heart, Jane knew Becca and Peter were soul mates and it was for the best. God had a way of working things out.

Thank goodness she'd had the wisdom to recognize that fact, even in the depths of her disappointment, for she had kept them both as her dearest friends.

But just maybe the time had arrived for her to find her own true love.

Indeed, it was not at all unlikely that at this very moment there was the possibility of having just as fine a fellow. A fellow who, if the truth be told, was even a mite more handsome. Although looks had certainly never been the deciding factor for her.

Her heart picked up pace as she looked down Main Street and conjured up a picture of the good-looking schoolmaster swinging around the corner and heading toward her office.

He would probably leave his buckboard at the church. It was a short walk, and it was such a beautiful day. The sun was bright but not yet glaring, and at the moment, a slight breeze was waving the stripes of the American flag flying above the post office across the street.

Certainly it was a day the Lord had made!

Even though Jane had not been able to attend service and hear Pastor Pike's sermon, she felt the Lord's presence just as keenly. In fact, she had taken a moment for her own private meditation as she did on these Sundays when she was on duty and couldn't attend church. She'd read from her Bible, which she always kept handy, right on her desk with her sheriff's manuals, to remind herself of a higher law.

That morning she'd turned to Psalm 96. "O sing unto the LORD a new song: sing unto the LORD, all the earth. Sing unto the LORD, bless his name; shew forth his salvation from day to day. Declare his glory among the heathen, his wonders among all people. For the LORD is great, and greatly to be praised."

Luke Thompson passed with his simpleminded son, Davy, on the seat beside him. Luke was a patient and loving father.

Should she go outside and greet John and Timmy?

She didn't want to seem too eager.

She glanced at her holster and gun, hanging on a hook by the door. Timmy would probably be real pleased to see her waiting for them, looking official with her badge and gun on. She still felt a little self-conscious in them, not like Papa who would have worn them in his sleep. And did often, leaning back in this very leather chair, with his feet up on the desk.

Those were not her proudest memories of Papa, although she wouldn't have admitted that to anyone, even her best friend. . .hardly to herself.

Outside on the boardwalk, she turned toward her reflection in the office window and pushed a recalcitrant blond strand of hair back from her brow. It was difficult to look like a serious public servant with such unruly curls.

She pinched her cheeks—she wished she had high color like Mary—and glanced over her shoulder.

Still no John and Timmy!

As she turned back, a slight movement caught her eye, enough to make her pause. . .and her blood suddenly run cold.

The door to the bank was gradually being pushed open.

On a Sunday?

Jane stepped back into the shadows, her heart pounding. Her hand went to her gun.

A bearded stranger stepped out carrying a canvas bag.

A flash of color to his right.

Oh, dear God. There was Timmy, skipping up the center of Main Street. Did the man see him?

An icy chill went up Jane's spine. In seconds they would converge.

"Stay back, Timmy! Stay back!" she called.

The man's head shot up. He looked in her direction.

In that instant, she recognized a likeness to the face on the WANTED poster she'd tacked on the post office wall. Could it be that missing member of the River Gang?

Timmy stopped in the middle of the street, confused.

"Run, Timmy!" she cried.

Too late!

Before Timmy could move, the man had stepped up and grabbed him from behind.

Timmy screamed, his arms flailing, his little legs kicking wildly.

Jane gasped. *Oh, dear God, no!* She stepped out of the shadows and leveled her gun. "Put the child down!"

At that same moment, John and Mary, carrying little Nancy, rounded the corner from First Street. It took but a breath, and John saw it all.

He lunged forward.

"Back away! Or the boy gets hurt." Clenching him in the crook of his left arm, the robber raised what looked like a long-barreled .45 to Timmy's head.

"Stay back, John. He means it," Jane screamed.

"Let the child go!" Mary cried out, her voice shrill with terror. "Oh please, let him go."

Startled, the man paused. He jerked his head in her direction. He seemed to falter.

Jane crouched, tense and waiting, her Peacemaker cocked, her finger curled around the trigger, the barrel still aimed at the marauder's head.

But with Timmy squirming, she couldn't take a chance.

They stood in the silent street as if in a play, each toeing his mark set by some phantom director: John to the side, poised to leap; Mary behind him, holding the baby; and in the middle of the street, the robber, clutching little Timmy, the lethal weapon at the child's temple.

The noonday sun beat down, hot and uncompromising. The air was thick, leaden with fear, hanging over them all like a transparent shroud.

Then, very deliberately, the man turned and swung the barrel of his .45 around, leveling the weapon directly at Mary and baby Nancy.

Jane fired.

The sharp report reverberated in the quiet street.

For a moment, the man stood transfixed, his mouth agape, a look of surprise on his hoary face. Then the pistol rolled from his fingers.

The baby started wailing.

Jane's hand began to shake. Slowly she lowered her gun as she watched blood spurting from the wound in the man's temple.

He staggered forward.

Timmy, tumbling from his grasp, ran screaming toward his father.

Slowly the robber slid to his knees, crumpled backward onto the ground, and lay still. His blood, pooling in the street, turned the clotted dust to crimson.

Locked in John's arms, Timmy's hysterical sobs, along with baby Nancy's startled crying, echoed in the eerie quiet.

Jane leaped down from the boardwalk and ran out to where the fallen man lay. She knelt down beside him, feeling for a pulse.

He was dead!

The rush of energy that had propelled her, drained.

"Thou shalt not kill" echoed in her brain.

But she had. She'd killed a man, another human being.

For the moment, she felt no remorse, only relief. She'd done what she had to do. Two lives, maybe three, had been saved.

She'd done her job.

She passed her hand over the silver gray, staring eyes, closing them to the hot rays of the unremitting sun.

"I think you should get the undertaker, John," she murmured.

Slowly she rose and, for a long moment, stared down at the man lying dead at her feet.

His high-styled, wool-checked suit was threadbare; the wing collar of his detailed shirt, frayed; and the patent leather tips of his expensive ankle boots were scuffed and worn.

Clearly the life this man once knew was not the life she had brought to an end.

twenty-one

Later, after John had hurried Timmy and Mary from the gruesome scene, after Booker Mortinson, the undertaker, had removed the body, Jane sat alone in her office, staring at the battered wallet on her desk, the wallet that had belonged to the dead man.

The man she had killed.

It had never occurred to her that she might actually have to shoot anyone. Not in Whispering Bluff, where the sheriff's job was, at worst, a matter of breaking up fights on a Saturday night.

Never could she have imagined the wrenching sadness that would come over her if, indeed, in the line of duty, she ever did have to kill another human being. Take the life of another living, breathing soul. A child of God! Yes, a child of God whether he chose to acknowledge it or not. He had been born to this world as one of God's precious creations, just as she had.

But he'd given her no choice.

None!

The man had aimed his gun directly at Mary and that dear baby girl. And all the while, he was holding Timmy, precious little Timmy.

She could only thank God that her aim had been true, that all her hours of practice had paid off.

But even as she had no guilt, she could not shake off the profound melancholy when she considered the life that had been so carelessly wasted in the interest of greed and evil.

But her job on this case was not finished yet.

She picked up the worn but expensive, hand-stitched wallet. It gave no clue to the man's identity, no name, no address inside. All that was in it were a few dirty bills and a tattered photograph.

She would send a telegraph to the surrounding counties, but she wondered if anyone would claim the body.

Oh so futile! So sad!

She sighed, picking up the photograph.

A dark, mustached man seated in a Victorian chair. She could barely see the resemblance to the squalid wastrel he'd become. He'd been handsome then. His bride stood behind him, her hand on his shoulder, beautiful, smiling, her dark hair framed by a pale lace mantilla.

The woman looked so much like. . .

No! It couldn't be!

She held the photograph up to the light.

Jane's heart leaped into her throat.

It was Mary.

Her own dear Mary!

How was it possible?

The crazy jumble of thoughts and recollections coursing through her brain made her weak.

But as they began to settle, it occurred to her how little she really did know about her friend, her past—her husband. Nothing, really, before Mary arrived in Whispering Bluff.

Now she understood why Mary had always been so vague. It appeared she had much to hide.

And yet when Mary had seen the WANTED poster she hadn't shown a quiver of recognition—nor had she as the man lay dead in the street.

Could she be that clever an actress?

Could all the goodness and sweetness that Jane had seen in her dear friend been only a charade?

No! She refused to believe that. It wasn't surprising that she hadn't recognized him. The man Jane had shot was seriously altered from the one in the picture.

But those cold steel eyes; how could one forget them?

And yet, if those eyes were a mirror of his evil soul, Jane could understand why Mary had run away and tried to lose herself in the safety of this remote little town. She could understand why she would choose Whispering Bluff.

But he had shown up, in the very town in which Mary had sought refuge.

It was a coincidence that begged explanation.

There was so much about Mary Smith that was a mystery. Was that even her name? Mary Smith?

The more Jane considered it all, the more depressed she became.

Then it struck her.

The photograph in her trembling hand held not only Mary's future but John's. . .and her own.

Had she never seen this picture—Mary would still be married. Jane would still have a chance to capture John's heart.

In a moment of utter disheartenment, she glanced from the photograph to the wastebasket beneath her desk.

twenty-two

As the afternoon sun melted into dusk, Mary rocked Nancy by the library window. Trembling at the thought of how differently this day might have ended, she bent and kissed the soft curls of her sleeping infant.

How close she had come to losing it all.

But, if what she'd experienced had been terrifying for her, how much more horrendous for Timmy. . .and John. And after the horrible tragedy they had already lived through.

She gazed across the book-lined room at the sleeping child, snuggled in the settee next to his father, his dear little tear-stained face peaceful at last in slumber. It had taken her and John until just a short time ago to calm him.

John looked up, and their gazes locked, the forbidden longing in his eyes reflecting the yearning in her own heart, made even more intense by the realization of how fragile life could be. How, even with God's protection, so many evil forces were in this universe to defy Him.

And with such frightful suddenness! This time it was a murderous bank robber. Who knew from whence the next threat might come.

At the sound of an approaching buggy, she turned and looked out the window.

"It's Jane," she murmured, rising. With Nancy in her arms, she hurried toward the door before Jane could knock and wake Timmy.

John gently disengaged himself from the sleeping child and followed.

With her finger to her lips, she ushered Jane into the kitchen. "Timmy's asleep," she explained quietly. Then observing her friend's troubled face, she put a comforting arm around her shoulders. "Oh, my dear, it has been a difficult day. How terribly distressing it must have been for you. But you were so brave. Our true heroine."

"You were indeed," John said. "And a sure shot, to boot, thank God." He crossed the kitchen and took her hand. "I have no doubt you likely saved at least three lives today. Certainly Mary's and little Nancy's." His voice broke with emotion. "And most probably my boy's."

For a moment, Jane looked slightly abashed. "It's my job. I just did what I had to do." Then her expression cleared and she withdrew her hand. "I'd appreciate it if you took Nancy into the parlor. Mary and I have to talk. Alone!"

It was not a request but a command, so abrupt and with such unaccustomed coolness that John at first looked startled.

"Of course." He shot her a quizzical look as he turned and lifted the baby from Mary's arms.

"What's this about?" Mary asked, bewildered.

Jane waited until John had disappeared down the hall. "You and I need to talk."

She gestured for Mary to take the chair across the kitchen table, pulled out the one opposite, and sat down. Very deliberately she folded her hands in front of her and gazed at Mary with such a penetrating, silent calm that Mary was set off balance—which, it seemed, was Jane's intention.

Why would that be?

A shiver of apprehension scurried up Mary's spine. Had Jane discovered her past, her endless trail of lies?

Desperately trying to remain calm, she waited.

But Jane was intent on taking her time, adding to Mary's discomfort.

Jane, the loquacious, the ebullient, suddenly just the opposite!

Finally Jane spoke. "Some things have transpired that seem to make it imperative that I learn more about you, Mary."

"What things are those?" Mary tried to keep her voice

composed, but a dreadful apprehension infused the very blood pulsing through her veins.

"We'll get to that. The point is, I've suddenly come to realize how very little I know about you."

There was a desperation in Mary now, a knowing, without knowing, that something dreadful was about to happen. She struggled to keep her tone level, innocent. "But, Janie, how can you say that? Why no one knows me better than you do."

"Only since the day you arrived in Whispering Bluff, the day before Christmas when you rode into town in your fancy phaeton wearing that rich, red velvet cloak." Jane remained immobile, her hands still locked in front of her, her gaze unwavering. "I'll never forget that cloak, crimson with a leopard-trimmed hood and cuffs. I know Mary Smith with the fashionable wardrobe and the finest house in Whispering Bluff. . . . Hardly affordable on a soldier's salary."

"I told you, I had an inheritance."

"And your parents are dead, as is the aunt who raised you. . . and you have no siblings. What did your father do, Mary, that he accumulated this fortune? Where did you come from? When did he and your mother die? What was his name. . .your maiden name? Where are the pictures of this family to which you owe so much? Where are the pictures of your devoted husband?"

For the first time, Jane lowered her eyes. She studied her clasped hands. "What amazes me is that I wasn't more curious, that I didn't even realize or notice. These are things that usually come out so naturally in as close a friendship as I thought we had."

"*Thought* we had?"

Jane shook her head and mused, "A whole lifetime in a satchel and a suitcase, and I wasn't even curious."

Mary jumped to her feet, transformed by a terrible fear. "Why are you asking me these questions? You're my dearest friend. Why are you treating me this way?"

What do you know? But she dared not ask.

Quietly Jane rose and drew a tintype from her pocket. She laid it on the kitchen table.

Mary looked down at the picture.

Her breath caught. She stared.

Clayton!

"Where did you get this?" she whispered.

"Then you don't deny you're the woman in the picture?"

What Mary had most feared had come to pass. Her lie had been exposed. Either her husband or the authorities in Chicago had caught up with her.

Now she'd be known for what she was, a criminal. . .possibly even a murderess.

Oh, dear God.

"You don't need to say anything, Mary; your expression says it all." Jane crossed her arms, studying her with narrowed assessment. "I found it in the wallet of the dead man."

"What?"

The events of the afternoon flashed before Mary: the robber's icy stare, the deliberation with which he turned and pointed his gun directly at her.

Should she have recognized him then? But how? If it were Clayton, his appearance was vastly altered.

No, it couldn't be!

But the eyes, those cold, menacing eyes. . .

She stared up at the ceiling, blinded by tears, unable to speak. Finally she managed to whisper, "I knew he'd gambled his fortune away, but I can't believe he would have resorted to bank robbery."

Jane didn't answer at once but continued her cool, speculative gaze. "It does seem ironic, doesn't it, that of all places, this is where he'd end up."

Mary looked at Jane, dumbstruck. "You don't think I had anything to do with it?"

"You tell me."

"No! I didn't—I wouldn't. I didn't even know if he was alive." Mary felt what little strength she had in her melt away. She caught hold of one of the ladder-back chairs for support. "All these months since I escaped, I was afraid I'd killed him."

"Killed him?" Jane's eyes widened.

Mary's spirit sank to even greater depths of despair. It didn't take a genius to see that she'd just given Jane information she hadn't been aware of. . .additional information with which to hang her.

Jane's usually soft lips were cast in a hard, straight line. "I think it's about time you told me the truth, Mary Smith. If that's your name."

How would Jane perceive her now—and the town, of which she'd become so much a part?

And John. Especially John!

It was all over. It would all come out. All of it! What would John think of her now, this woman with whom he had entrusted his most prized possession? His son.

"I think we should call John in," she whispered.

"You're sure you want that?"

Mary nodded, sagging into the chair.

"Very well." Jane's voice was flat. Far from the lilting soprano that Mary knew. "You're probably right. He probably should hear this."

A minute later, Jane reappeared carrying Nancy, John following her. She settled the baby in the high chair and turned. "Sit down, John."

Mary had never heard her friend sound so much like a sheriff. She spoke in a voice that gave no quarter.

It frightened her even more.

"I found this on the dead man." Jane pushed the photograph across the table.

Mary couldn't look at John. She set her gaze on her clenched hands in her lap.

After what seemed forever, he finally spoke. "This is you," he mumbled.

She lifted her head. "He was my husband."

Nancy's playful gurgling struck a dissonant note in the quiet room.

"His name was Clayton Rockford."

Jane kept coldly mute, waiting for her to continue.

Waiting for me to dig my own grave.

"I'm Marybelle Rockford." She pushed herself up from the table. "So, there you have it. It's all been a big lie. There's no husband off fighting a war."

Neither Jane nor John spoke.

Mary felt the barrier of their silence.

"I prayed I could live out my life here in peace, with no one the wiser." She couldn't hide her bitterness. "Now I see that it never will be. Even with his death, I can't escape him."

Sighing, she dropped back into her chair. "I thought I'd found a home here, a place where I fit in—where Nancy and I fit in. I was a new person with a new name."

She took them both in with a glance. "I know you think I've deceived you, and I have. But I didn't know what else to do."

Their silence was dreadful. She thought she'd drown in it. She looked down at her clasped hands and began again.

Haltingly, her voice evidence of an anguish she couldn't control, she poured out the story of her marriage: of how her husband had squandered his fortune and much of hers in drunken debauchery and infidelity, of his extreme and violent physical abuse.

But would they believe her?

She touched the scar on her cheek.

"It got so I didn't even care what happened to me. If he'd killed me, it would almost have been a blessing. And then I found out I was going to have a child. That's when I made up my mind to leave him. I couldn't risk my baby's life."

She was choking back sobs. "He came home early and

found me packing. He was so angry. Like a madman. Worse than he had ever been. He struck me, over and over. He was choking me. I grabbed the bedside lamp and hit him, and I hit him. . . . When I ran out, I didn't know if he was alive or dead. And worst of all, God help me, I didn't care."

She dropped her head on her folded arms, weak with sadness and despair.

But also with relief.

The wondering, the pretending, the fear of discovery were finally over.

For what seemed an eternity, neither Jane nor John responded.

Why should they? What was there to say?

"Why didn't you tell me?" Jane asked finally, her sweet voice trembling with emotion.

Mary lifted her eyes. "How could I? For all I knew, I could have been a murderess. I waited for the day when I'd see my own face on one of those posters."

"Without a beard, I trust," John murmured. His words were light, but the eyes he turned on her were quite the opposite. They bespoke of his compassion and understanding. . .and more. So much more that Mary's heart began to lift with hope.

Was it possible he didn't hate her?

"It makes me sad," he said, his voice husky with the depth of his emotion. "It makes me sad that you didn't know you could confide in me, that you felt you had to bear this alone."

Tears welled in Mary's eyes. "What's going to happen to Nancy and me now?"

If only one of them would leap into the breach of silence.

Oh, John.

She stared down at her clasped hands.

Finally he did speak, his voice reluctant, distracted. "Whatever happens, you and Nancy won't be alone." That was all he said, no more, only sighed heavily and stood.

It was his kind heart speaking. Why should she expect more? Essentially she'd lied to him, not in what she'd said but in what she'd left unsaid. In that sense, she'd lied to them both.

But not in her heart! Never in her heart!

Couldn't he see that?

He was pacing now, pausing by the kitchen window, looking absently out over her garden, through the copse of trees to his own house.

His lonely house, she thought.

Just as hers would be lonely without him, oh so lonely without him!

"This is a lot to throw at a man all at once," he muttered, more to himself than to her or Jane. For the moment, he seemed hardly aware of either of them.

As wretched and silent as Mary sat, so sat Jane across from her.

There was misery all around them. It permeated the air. It was leaden in their hearts. Even Nancy sensed it as she fretted and reached out for her mother.

Mary felt as old and broken as an ancient urn, a vessel of no further use. She willed herself to rise, to put one foot in front of the other, to move across the polished pine floor to her baby, to reach out and lift her—this heavy, precious burden whose life, whose whole future depended on her.

She turned.

John was standing there, facing her, looking down at her, his sad gaze locked with hers. Wordlessly he reached out and wrapped his arms around her and drew her close, drew her and Nancy close against his heart. He rested his cheek against her hair.

"We'll make it, Mary. Together we'll make it."

She closed her eyes, trembling in his arms.

Was it true? Was she hearing what she thought she heard or what she so desperately wanted to hear—needed to hear?

"Don't worry, my darling. You and Nancy are safe now. You're safe." The words repeated like a mantra as he stroked her hair and held her close.

Until Nancy began to squirm between them, poking with little knees and elbows and tiny feet. She let out a fretful cry, and Mary and John were thrown back into the reality of the moment; he released her, smiling down at her with his heart in his eyes, and she smiling back as if no one else in the world existed.

Suddenly guilt washed over her, and she turned her gaze to Jane's sweet, thoughtful face and wondered if John could possibly know the sad price that Jane was paying for her discovery.

Mary watched her friend take a fortifying breath. "I think what happens next," Jane said slowly, "is that Mary Smith will be receiving a telegram from the department of the army, informing her that her husband has been killed in action." Jane stood. "Which, in a sense, is true."

"Oh, Jane. . ."

"You have become my dearest friend, Mary. I see no reason to give the gossips full rein. What has come to light today stays"—she touched her heart—"here." Then she smiled, no longer the sheriff. "Provided Nancy keeps her little mouth closed."

With that surprising levity, she turned and headed for the door.

Mary followed her out to her buggy, leaving John to watch Nancy. "Jane—"

Jane held up her hand. "If you're going to say what I think you're going to say, don't!"

"What do you think I was going to say?"

Jane's face took on a pensive look as she grasped Mary's hand. "I've seen the way John looks at you. . .and whether you realize it or not, the way you look at him. You belong with each other." She smiled ruefully. "My interest in John was but a hopeful fancy. A fancy in my heart alone, most assuredly, never in his! I knew that all along. But given the circumstances. . ." She shrugged. "No, my dear, you were the one from the beginning. And you always will be."

Blinking back tears, Mary leaned over and kissed Jane on the cheek. "You are my truest friend."

Later, with Nancy tucked in bed and Timmy still napping on the library couch, Mary and John sat out on the back steps under the stars. The air was warm and redolent with the scent of night-blooming jasmine.

Mary felt light-headed, almost giddy, sitting so close to him. She could feel his warmth through the delicate fabric of her blouse and the strength of his muscled arm around her shoulders.

John chuckled. "These past weeks, I've been fantasizing about what I would say to you if only I could, if only I were free to. If only you weren't a married woman. And now you aren't, and here I am, tongue-tied as a callow youth." He shook his head. "And I call myself a poet."

"Oh, John." She leaned her head against his shoulder, laughter welling up inside her. "And all this time, I've looked into your kind, handsome face, wishing I could hear such words but reminding myself that I was a married woman—or a killer." She reached up and touched his cheek.

It had probably been one of the most difficult and tumultuous days of her life. But in this moment of repose, she breathed a silent prayer of gratitude to the Almighty, for she had found a peace and contentment beyond her most impossible dream.

John turned and held her close—so close she felt his heart beating in rhythm with her own.

No words were needed now.

Gently his lips traced the contours of hers, tentative at first, and then with increasing warmth and pressure as they poured into that kiss all the pent-up passion that for so long had sought release.

epilogue

Mary and John were married the following spring, Pastor Pike officiating. The simple little prairie church was crowded. Jane, Mary's one attendant, smiled bravely through the ceremony, hiding the tears Mary knew were still in her heart.

Just before the service began, five-year-old Timmy stood at attention in front of the altar, wearing the charming little white sailor outfit Mavis Dodd had fashioned just for him. His arms hung rigidly at his sides, his large, dark eyes focused straight ahead.

The sanctuary fell silent as he opened his little-boy mouth and began to sing a cappella, all five verses of "Now the Day Is Over," ending with " 'When the morning wakens, then may I arise, pure and fresh and sinless in Thy holy eyes.' Amen." It was the hymn the children's choir at the Good Shepherd Community Church had just learned—and Timmy's choice—sung with such sweet, pure perfection that when he had finished, it didn't matter that it was hardly appropriate for a wedding. There was nary a dry eye in the little church.

At the altar, Mary held Nancy's tiny hand. Her toddler seemed to understand the solemnity of the occasion and kept her squirming to a minimum. Timmy stood beside John, his own little hand locked in his father's warm grasp.

Afterward everyone gathered in the parsonage, decorated by the garden club with the ladies' loveliest spring flowers. The table was laden with the sweetest treats from Jane's and Pru's larders.

As Mary's gaze passed over her friends, her heart was so full of love and gratitude it took her breath away. God had surely watched over her and answered her prayers in ways she could never have imagined.

Only for a moment did her mind drift back to her prior wedding in the great cathedral, banked with a profusion of garlands and grand bouquets, full of pomp and circumstance, crowded with people. Many of them strangers!

The sum total of that congregation's caring was less than from the heart of one of her dear friends in this room.

That marriage had ended at the wedding. This wedding was the beginning of a marriage.

A blessedly love-filled marriage!

A Letter To Our Readers

Dear Reader:

In order that we might better contribute to your reading enjoyment, we would appreciate your taking a few minutes to respond to the following questions. We welcome your comments and read each form and letter we receive. When completed, please return to the following:

Fiction Editor
Heartsong Presents
PO Box 719
Uhrichsville, Ohio 44683

1. Did you enjoy reading *Alias, Mary Smith* by Rachel Druten?
   ❑ Very much! I would like to see more books by this author!
   ❑ Moderately. I would have enjoyed it more if

   _____

   _____

   _____

2. Are you a member of **Heartsong Presents**? ❑ Yes ❑ No
   If no, where did you purchase this book? _____

   _____

3. How would you rate, on a scale from 1 (poor) to 5 (superior), the cover design? _____

4. On a scale from 1 (poor) to 10 (superior), please rate the following elements.

____	Heroine	____	Plot
____	Hero	____	Inspirational theme
____	Setting	____	Secondary characters

5. These characters were special because? _____

_____

_____

6. How has this book inspired your life? _____

_____

_____

7. What settings would you like to see covered in future
   Heartsong Presents books? _____

_____

_____

8. What are some inspirational themes you would like to see
   treated in future books? _____

_____

_____

9. Would you be interested in reading other **Heartsong
   Presents** titles? ❏ Yes ❏ No

10. Please check your age range:
    ❏ Under 18   ❏ 18-24
    ❏ 25-34   ❏ 35-45
    ❏ 46-55   ❏ Over 55

Name _____

Occupation _____

Address _____

City, State, Zip_____

DIAMOND DUO

Lose yourself in this gripping historical romance, where an alluring stranger incites passion, betrayal, and murder. Based on an actual unsolved murder in Jefferson, Texas by author Marcia Gruver.

Historical, paperback, 320 pages, 5³/₁₆" x 8"

_____

Presents

Great Inspirational Romance at a Great Price!

Heartsong Presents books are inspirational romances in contemporary and historical settings, designed to give you an enjoyable, spirit-lifting reading experience. You can choose wonderfully written titles from some of today's best authors like Wanda E. Brunstetter, Mary Connealy, Susan Page Davis, Cathy Marie Hake, Joyce Livingston, and many others.

When ordering quantities less than twelve, above titles are $2.97 each.
Not all titles may be available at time of order.